JF HOMZIE
Homzie, Hillary, author.
Apple pie promises

W9-BGD-871

URL UP WITH ALL OF THE SWIRL NOVELS!

Apple Pie Promises

APPLE PIE PROMISES

Hillary Homzie

Fountaindale Public Library
Bolingbrook, IL
(630) 759-2102

Sky Pony Press
New York

Copyright © 2018 by Hillary Homzie

All rights reserved. No part of this book may be reproduced in any manner without the express written consent of the publisher, except in the case of brief excerpts in critical reviews or articles. All inquiries should be addressed to Sky Pony Press, 307 West 36th Street, 11th Floor, New York, NY 10018.

First edition

This is a work of fiction. Names, characters, places, and incidents are from the author's imagination, used fictitiously.

Sky Pony Press books may be purchased in bulk at special discounts for sales promotion, corporate gifts, fund-raising, or educational purposes. Special editions can also be created to specifications. For details, contact the Special Sales Department, Sky Pony Press, 307 West 36th Street, 11th Floor, New York, NY 10018 or info@skyhorsepublishing.com.

Sky Pony® is a registered trademark of Skyhorse Publishing, Inc.®, a Delaware corporation.

Visit our website at www.skyponypress.com.

10 9 8 7 6 5 4 3 2 1

Library of Congress Cataloging-in-Publication Data is available on file.

Cover design by Kate Gartner
Cover photos credit iStock

Paperback ISBN: 978-1-5107-3923-9
Ebook ISBN: 978-1-5107-3924-6

Printed in the United States of America

Chapter One
THE MOUNTAIN ISN'T OUT

I know they say an apple a day is good for you. Personally, I prefer my apple inside of a pie. And not just any pie, but one that I'm baking.

There is nothing like the smell of a buttery piecrust and cinnamon-tossed apples. It says that the world is good, even after your parents have been arguing, or your braces have been tightened, or an entire mountain range of zits have just erupted on your face, or the boy you've had a crush on since sixth grade still doesn't know you exist.

That's the power of pie.

That's why I'm smiling right now. Because Mom and I are baking one.

It's not officially fall, but it's close, since it's towards the end of August. It's an overcast Saturday morning and there's a definite chill in the air.

We use two varieties of apples: Honeycrisp because they are sweet and sturdy and Granny Smith because they're tart and refreshing. This keeps everything balanced. If you use too many Honeycrisps, the sugariness will take over. If you use too many Granny Smiths, the pie will become tart and bitter. It's all about finding that perfect balance.

"This pie is going to be awesome," I say, slicing across the bottom of an apple core.

"Mmmm," agrees Mom. Only she sounds far away, like she's thinking about her next group project or research paper. Mom is finishing up her master's degree in public health at the University of Washington (a.k.a. U-Dub), which means she commutes a couple of times a week from Tacoma (where we live) into Seattle.

Using a paring knife, she peels her apple into thick threads. "So I want to talk to you about something." Her voice suddenly sounds bright and eager.

"I know! You want us to enter an apple pie into the baking contest this year at the Fall Festival."

My middle school sponsors the festival as a fundraiser in mid-October. It's really fun, raises money for the P.T.A., and everyone goes. There are hayrides, carnival games, a cakewalk, even a haunted house. The contests are an especially big deal—the winners get awesome gift cards! Last year, I didn't enter because I thought it was something only the eighth graders did. But anyone can enter, including seventh graders like me.

"Is that what it's about?" I ask because she weirdly hasn't answered me. "The pie contest."

"Not exactly, although entering is a great idea. You're becoming quite the baker, Lily."

Mom pushes her dark hair off her forehead. Like me, she's good at staying neat, so I'm surprised to see strands of hair sticking out of her ponytail. She haphazardly slices her apples, creating a mix of half-centimeter and full-centimeter slices.

Alarmed, I glance at the mess of apples. "Mom, they're too thick. And too thin."

"What? Oh. It's fine." Her smile is extra bright. With her long hair and freckled nose, she looks like a carefree teenager. But she's not. She's thirty-five and a worrier. So the way she's acting right now makes no sense. She's always reminding me that texture is everything with a pie. If the slices are too thin, the texture is off. Too thick and the pie will feel chunky.

"There's something I've been meaning to tell you." She sets down the knife and scoops the apple pieces into a colander. "I won the fellowship!" she trills.

"What are you talking about?"

"Someone dropped out of the program. So as the alternate, I'm going to Morocco for a year in her place!"

"What?! They can't do this to you! It's *so* last minute. They can't tell you no, then suddenly yes. They should have picked you in the first place." Last fall, Mom had applied to a yearlong fellowship in Rabat, Morocco, to help organize a conference on women's rights and health. She was excited about it because her grandfather was Moroccan, but she knows very little about the culture and wants to learn.

"You told them no, right?"

"I said yes."

"Mom, how could you?! There's no time." My heart pulses in my ears.

"There's over two weeks."

"How am I going to get ready, or tell my friends goodbye?"

"Don't worry. You're not going with me." She jostles the colander as if she can bang the juice right out of the apples. "We went over this last year. It's a twelve-month fellowship in the capital. I'll be living in a very small apartment, and I'm going to be working twenty-four seven. It's just not set up for families."

"How long have you known?" My voice is shrieky even in my own ears.

"Honey, I just got the phone call." A giant smile grows on my mom's face. She seems super happy about leaving her only kid. "And it just worked out."

"Worked out?"

"We'll be in constant contact and you'll be with your dad."

"Yeah, and his new-and-improved family." A couple of weeks ago, I got back from spending two months with my dad, and now I have to go back? My hands tremble, and my mom looks pale. Probably because I'm implying that my stepmother is an improvement over her. And that's not true. My hand cups my mouth. Usually I'm good about keeping mean things inside.

But not today.

Mom is seriously the most incredible person I know. She works full-time as an administrator at a women's health clinic, goes to school, and always has time for me. Plus, she doesn't ever completely lose it. She wasn't always that way, though.

Before my parents got divorced, they fought a lot. It wasn't good. And I promised myself I would never ever be like them. I would never explode or argue. I'd keep my feelings safely inside.

I remember my parents getting into a huge argument on the plane when we were traveling to see my grandma in Virginia. Unfortunately, they were sitting on either side of me, and I couldn't pretend to need to go to the bathroom because the seat belt sign was on.

It was bad. It was loud. It was embarrassing. And it was all about leaving a cell phone charger in the airport waiting area.

Dad had waved his arms.

Mom had thrown an entire packet of mini pretzels. I later found a pretzel in my hair.

Everyone around us had stared, including the very cute boy across the aisle. I vowed that I would never lose control like that. I would be legendary for my calmness.

"I'm sorry, Mom," I say softly. And *very* calmly. "I didn't mean it. I wasn't expecting this. To live with Dad full-time and for you to be away. *Very* away."

"I know." Color returns to her face. "Lily, remember to live like the mountain is out."

I nod and try not to cry. It's a saying we have in Tacoma. It means to live like it's a clear sunny day, when you can see Mount Rainer, which looms snow-peaked over the city. Sometimes you can't see the mountain because of the weather, but you know it's close by. This situation is way different, though. Mom will truly be far away.

Suddenly, I'm dying to talk my best friend, Keisha. She'll be super surprised that Mom would leave so last minute, since, like me, Mom's a planner.

This year, Mom and I were supposed to enter our pie and win first place.

She was going to show me how to knit.

The only thing I was supposed to worry about was whether Ethan Sanarov, a super awesome eighth grader who I've been afraid to talk to, could be more than just a secret crush.

This year wasn't supposed to be like this.

As soon as I can, I text Keisha and tell her to meet me at Jefferson Park by the giant sequoia. I let her know it's urgent. The tree is our usual spot. It's far away from the little kids in the water spray area and the playground.

Listening to the *shush-shush* of the sprinklers in the water park, I watch for Keisha. It feels like it takes forever, but I finally see her ride up and dump her bike in the nearby grassy field. I hurriedly motion for her to sit next to me.

When she races over, it takes everything I have to hold back my tears. Keisha's wearing a pair of shorts and a t-shirt with sequins that says *Girl Squad*. I'm in the rattiest pair of sweats ever and a hole-infested tie-dye shirt from camp because I didn't have time to change.

When Keisha asks me what's going on, I do my best to fill her in on the details without crying.

After giving me a huge hug, she gives me her intense Keisha eye lock and grabs my hands. "It's going to be hard being separated from your mom. That's some rough stuff."

"I know." I sniffle but I don't cry.

"You got this, Lily. Seriously. You can do anything." She pauses.

"Thanks," I whisper.

"But if you want to scream, go ahead. You'll just scare some leaves off the trees."

Even though I have a lump wedged in my throat, I snort.

Suddenly Keisha points and shrieks. "Look! There's Ethan. He's playing basketball."

"Are you serious?" I feel my eyes bug as I steal a glance at my ratty sweatpants.

"Actually, I lied. I just said that to cheer you up some more. I hated seeing you look so sad."

"Well, hearing that Ethan—*The* Ethan—Mr. Beautiful Ethan with his shiny blond swimmer hair is standing in the same park when I'm looking like pond scum doesn't make me happy!"

"Sorry. It was meant to be a get-to-your-happy-place thought." She peers at my torn-up tie-dye t-shirt. It's not like me to just thrown any old thing on and she knows it. Usually, I like to put some thought into what I wear. "I freaked you out," says Keisha with a sigh. "How about this happy thought? You can video chat and email with your mom. And probably call a whole bunch."

"Yes, but it's not the same! Look, it's not like I don't love my dad, it's different."

"At least Kimberly's nice. You've even said so yourself. And Hannah's, um, interesting."

Dad and Kimberly met on some dating app last summer. (A dating app that I showed him how to use! When it comes to phones, he's normally clueless.) That fall, he introduced me to Kimberly and her daughter Hannah, who I already semi-knew because she's a year ahead of me at Carlton Middle, a huge school where it's hard to actually know the kids who are in different grades. Well, other than by reputation. But Hannah, with purple streaks in hair, is hard to miss. She's known for her creativity. But not her modesty. Somehow she manages to do theater, excel at art, and is a very competitive swimmer.

On the other hand, I'm not a superstar at anything. Unlike Hannah, I don't go to some special camp for the gifted and talented. I'm nice. I'm not popular but I'm not unpopular, either. I play the flute and like pie baking. Oh, and I do well in school, not because I'm some genius, but because I always do my homework, and I try really hard.

Grades are probably the only area where I beat Hannah. I've overheard Kimberly complain that Hannah's grades are uneven. We all know Hannah is smart, but somehow, she's always behind on assignments.

I'm never been behind on anything. I'm not the kind of person who can improvise or do anything the last minute so I like to stay on schedule.

In the fall, I'll start seventh grade and Hannah will be in eighth, so we're pretty much in different worlds.

Last April, Dad moved out of his apartment and into Kimberly's townhouse, and then they got married in May. Which meant I had a chance to have a lot of awkward dinners with Hannah, but hardly any alone time with her since it was always the four of us. Plus, over the summer, Hannah was away at camp and visiting relatives, so we've never actually lived together.

"I think calling Hannah interesting is being really generous," I say to Keisha. "More like unfriendly. And how about just plain rude?" The few times we've hung out, Hannah was either on her phone or drawing on her iPad. She's seemed completely uninterested in me, like she was pretending I didn't exist.

"Well, she *is* older, and last year we were just sixth graders," says Keisha. "Maybe now that you're about to be a seventh grader, it'll be different. Think about how well everything went this summer when you were living at your dad's."

"Yeah, because Hannah was away at art camp."

"Things will change once you get a chance to really know her."

"You sound just like my mom."

"That's because I'm awesome. And she's awesome."

"I know," I say. It's true. Keisha's always been there for me, and so has Mom.

My mom is a seriously supportive person.

She helped me when I quit tae kwon do to focus on playing the flute. When I thought I lost Keisha because of a stupid misunderstanding. When I needed wrist surgery and couldn't go on our sixth-grade class field trip to the Woodland Park Zoo, instead we went to a paint-your-own-ceramic place and made supercool zoo plates. The list of her awesomeness is endless.

And that's exactly why I don't want her to go away.

The sky is vanilla white.

When I look up, there's no sun or mountain in sight.

Chapter Two
TAKEOFFS AND PROMISES

Two weeks later, I'm standing with Mom at Sea-Tac Airport in front of international departures. It's Labor Day weekend and the airport is mobbed. Uber drivers and shuttle buses load and unload. Dad's circling around so we have time to say our goodbye.

Mom has two large suitcases as well as a carry-on. She holds out her phone and takes a selfie with me.

She's smiling, beaming actually, and I'm not. Well, I'm trying to be happy, but I know it looks forced.

"I can't believe this is happening," she says over the roar of planes taking off and landing.

Neither can I. "Will you send me the photo?" I ask.

"Of course."

"You might not have Wi-Fi on the plane."

"Doing it now." Mom taps her phone. "Sent."

She gives me a huge hug and I don't want to let her go. My throat feels thick. "I'm happy for you, Mom," I say. And that's true, at least partly.

"This is something I've dreamed about forever. I'm still pinching myself. It's like waking up and realizing you're getting that gold on the other side of the rainbow."

For as long as I can remember, she's always wanted to travel and work internationally, especially in Morocco.

She shakes her head with an awestruck expression. "Always go for it, Lily. Never give up. Never. Even when it seems like everything's against you." Her cheeks are Jonathan apple red. She's seriously glowing.

"I won't," I say, thinking about how Mom got pregnant with me when she was a senior in college, and she told me how hard it was to finish her degree. But she did it.

She smoothes a strand of hair behind my ear. "Honey, I get this isn't . . . this isn't going to be easy for you. But I know you're strong and will learn a lot." She places her arm around my shoulder. "Let's look at this way: I want to go. I don't want you to be miserable. This will be an opportunity to try new things, make stronger bonds—starting with your stepsister."

"Yeah, I guess that part's good."

"More than good. Great! Hannah's so creative. You could have fun together. You know those watercolor pencils Grandma sent you? You two can do that together. Or maybe make an About Me collage. Or greeting cards to mail to a certain person who's going to be overseas—*hint hint*. And you know Kimberly's nice. Maybe you can show her and Hannah how to bake."

"Yeah, maybe. I don't know if they're into that sort of thing."

Some guy jumps out of a van and practically runs over my toes with his luggage.

"It'd just be another way to get close," continues Mom. "I understand Kimberly's really into scrapbooking. Maybe she can help you decorate your room. She has a wonderful design sense. I think you all will have a great time! And they just got that cute dog."

"Maybe," I say, and somehow my mom's enthusiasm is working a little bit. Thinking about Maisie, an adorable goldendoodle, helps.

Unclenching my hands, I give a tentative smile.

"Try to really make this new"—she pauses—"living situation all work out." She looks so earnest, so hopeful as she reaches out a hand to me, that I can't help but feel hopeful, too. "Promise me you'll try your very best."

Ugh. My family isn't very good at promises. First of all, with my parents, the have-and-to-hold-until-death-do-us-part didn't exactly happen. And there are the little things. My dad promised me that he would rent an RV and we would go to Yellowstone. It's never happened. My mom promised me I could get my ears double pierced. Then she said I had to wait until I was older, in case I changed my mind. Blah blah blah.

But I can't be like that.

"I will." I take Mom's hand. It's warm and strong. "I promise."

"Good." Her smile grows even bigger as she gives my hand a squeeze. Wow. She's so happy. Seeing her like this makes my heart lift.

I'm really going to try and live like the mountain is out. For Mom.

Chapter Three
NOT IN THE PLANS

An hour after I've said goodbye to Mom at the airport, my own suitcase clacks along the sidewalk as I wheel it forward. The sky is periwinkle blue and it's a warm Sunday morning on Labor Day weekend. The perfect weather is making me feel guilty for being in a bad mood. Mom left for an entire year, and now I'm about to live with Dad and his new family. Just like Mom, a selection of my belongings are all packed away and ready for a new home.

I've checked my planner five times to make sure that I haven't left anything behind.

Okay, correction. I've left a lot of stuff behind since my dad's place is small. Basically, I had to choose only my favorite items to take, such as few of my favorite books, an entire manga action romance series, a few stuffed animals, candles, and some of my favorite framed photos.

I think about my pledge to my mom to make living at my dad's work. I'm certainly going to try. But I have a strange, unsettled feeling in the pit of my stomach. I grab my phone and text Keisha: *I'm here. Wish me luck.*

Keisha replies: *It's going to be fine.*

Me: *I hope so!*

Keisha: *I know so! xoxo*

A carry-on bag digs into my shoulder.

My dad wheels another one of my suitcases and he's already at the front door. He's wearing a pair of gym shorts and a Dave Matthews Band t-shirt. I can't help but notice he looks a lot trimmer. He used to be on the verge of pudgy. His blondish-reddish beard is neatly trimmed. Mom used to always beg for him to be more physically active. Kimberly has obviously been a good influence on him. Now I can sort of see why Keisha thinks he's cute for a dad.

"Home sweet home," he says, gesturing at the house.

I know he's trying to be positive, but it's not my home. Not really. I love my dad. But until recently he traveled so much for work (his latest job was in office supply sales), he was more like a classic weekend dad. We'd see the latest *Star Wars*, play miniature golf, or hike Swan Creek Park, and, sure, we always have fun, but Mom's my center. She's the one who brings in bags of tangerines for snacks for school dances, takes me to my orthodontist appointments, and bakes with me.

After rolling my suitcase up the steps, I cross the threshold of the gray-shingled townhouse. My stepmother, Kimberly, has opened the door for Dad ahead of me, and rushes to give me a hug. She's in a matching two-piece sweatpants outfit. (She's a matchy-matchy sort of person.) Her short blonde hair is neatly coiffed.

"Welcome, Lily," she says brightly. "Can I help you bring in your things?" She sounds genuinely pleased to see me. That's a good thing.

"I think we have everything," says Dad. "I already put your luggage back in the bedroom."

"Maisie. No," Kimberly says as a giant rust-colored goldendoodle bounds toward the doorway.

I'm so happy to see the new dog! But Kimberly grabs Maisie by the collar. "Inside. You'll get your walk in a minute. But you need something called a leash, you silly."

Maisie jumps up on me as I try to pull my suitcase into the living room.

"Down, puppy," says Kimberly. Maisie is actually not a puppy. She's two and a half. But nobody has told her that. "I'm sorry. She's just super excited to see you."

"It's okay," I say.

Maisie now has her paws around my middle like she wants to dance.

Kimberly laughs nervously. "Bad dog," she says. But you can tell she thinks it's almost cute. Last year, my sixth-grade math teacher, Ms. Drummond, was like that with some of the boys. She'd tell them to cut joking around, but you could see the smile in her eyes. It was so annoying.

Maisie continues jumping, and I subtly knee her away, but not hard. I like dogs, and I hate the idea of hurting her, but still—nobody has disciplined this dog for even one nanosecond.

"She really needs her walk," says Kimberly, and she grabs a leash. "Are you sure you all don't need help?"

"I'm fine." Okay, that's a lie.

Already I feel like a visitor. I remember that's how it was during the summer, which is Dad-time per the custody agreement. I was living with Mom more full-time during the school year, except for some weekends, but during June and July it had just been me, Dad, and Kimberly. In June, Hannah stayed with her grandparents down in Orange County in Southern California. Her dad died when she was really little, and she spends a whole month down there with her father's family. Then in July she went to this hippie art camp. And since my dad and Kimberly had just gotten married, they were in their honeymoon phase, which meant they were all touchy-feely with each other.

Right now my throat feels too tight. I'm missing my mom and it's just been a little more than an hour since we said goodbye. We only had a chance to spend a month together before she left.

This doesn't feel like when she went away to Boston to help my Aunt Ginger take care of her newborn twins.

Or when she left for a friends' long weekend in the nearby San Juan Islands. For both of those times, I knew she would return really soon.

Now it's going to be twelve months before she flies back home.

"Okay, then," says Kimberly, smiling at Maisie. "I'm going to take this monster on a walk. Otherwise, she's going to go crazy. Aren't you, Maisie Waisie?" She clips on her leash. "Oh, Lily, I bought you baking supplies. I know how much you like to bake."

"Thanks," I say. This is new. And surprising in a good way. In the summer, when Kimberly was on the Paleo Diet, there definitely wasn't any flour or sugar in the house. I guess she's being more flexible now.

"I also got some blueberries from the farmers' market," she says, heading toward the door. "They're on the first shelf in the fridge. I know they're your favorite. Please feel free to help yourself." Smiling, she looks hopeful and eager.

"That's awesome," I say, like it's the greatest thing ever. I actually do like blueberries. It's not like I'm some blueberry fanatic, though. But I don't want to disappoint her.

Maisie pulls Kimberly through the doorway. "We'll be back soon," she says with a wave. "Somebody *really* needs a walk."

"The question is: Who is walking who?" Dad says with a wink as he heads back to his SUV. "I think we left your pillows in the back."

"Right." I'm really particular about my pillows. They can't be filled with feathers because I'm allergic, but they have to feel like feathers. And they can't be all puffy and foamy. They need to sink down. We open the back of the SUV, but the pillows aren't there.

"I must have forgotten them," I moan.

"That isn't like you, Lily." Dad scratches his head, which is mostly bald, except for a half-moon of hair at the back, which he keeps in a buzz cut.

It's true. I remember everything for both of us. I have lists. "Can you go back to Mom's apartment?" I ask hopefully. She's leasing it to a friend of hers while we're gone.

"We have plenty of extra pillows. It'll be fine. We can get them another time."

I want to snap—*no, it's not fine. I need my own pillows. The squishy kind.* But I don't want to sound like some spoiled only child, so I follow him back inside.

In the living room, there are photos of a younger Hannah with a pageboy haircut and sweet smile. Was she ever really sweet or was it all an act? And then I remember that I haven't seen Hannah yet.

"Is, um, Hannah around?" I ask.

"She has swim practice. She'll be back soon."

Good. I feel a little burst of anticipation. Sure, maybe when we hung out before, Hannah seemed distant and acted a little superior, but we've hardly had time to get to know each other. And we like the same Netflix shows. Plus, she was semi-nice at the wedding back in May, showing me how she made her own bouquet and how to make one myself. Maybe it's all going to work out just fine.

I will actually have a sister. I feel myself starting to relax. My chest doesn't feel as tight. When I was little, I used to wish on every star for a sister. Two sisters, actually. I wanted a younger one to boss around and an older sister to show me the ropes.

Okay, I'm ready for all of this, I think. Mom would be proud.

While Kimberly is on her walk with Maisie, Dad and I sit outside in the backyard and talk about his memories of seventh grade.

"It was the best year ever of because of this thing called open classrooms," he says. " It basically just meant you could do your own thing. So my buddy Matt and I played hangman and paper football. It was awesome!"

"Dad, you're supposed to be telling me how hard you studied."

"Then I'd be lying," he says, chuckling. "My life's an example for you not to follow." His phone buzzes. "Oh! Got to get ready for a shoot." Dad recently started a business filming high school sports, and things are really taking off. A few different school districts have asked him to shoot videos, so he's already had to hire freelancers. He slaps his forehead. "I can't keep up with everything. Want to tag along?"

"I'd love to, Dad, but I really need to unpack."

"But it's such a beautiful day. It's Tacoma. You have to seize the moment."

I frown because I'd love to be outside. "I've got to stick to my plan." In fact, it's actually written down in my planner in purple permanent ink. **TODAY UNPACK!!!!**

"Then why don't we go apple picking next weekend?" says Dad. "Just the two of us."

"That's a great idea! I'd love to do that. It'd be awesome to bake with super fresh apples." I give Dad a hug. "Thanks! I'll go write it down in my planner."

"You and Kimberly are two peas in pod," says Dad. "Planners, not procrastinators." It's weird and a little annoying how Dad is accepting of Kimberly being organized but not into Mom wanting things neat. Does it mean he's changed or is it he just so in love? "One day, you'll rub off on me," he continues. As a joke, he literally rubs his hand over his beard. "Tell you what. How about on my way back from filming, I'll pick up some pizza at Abella?"

Despite my annoyance, I grin. It's our favorite place. "Some pepperoni and pineapple?"

"Perfect. And I'll get some artichoke and pesto for Kimberly."

He leaves just as Kimberly returns from her walk with Maisie. Back in the living room, I avert my head as they kiss. Even though it's not a long one, it feels like it should be private.

Kimberly offers me a tour of the kitchen, which seems odd since I stayed there for most of the summer, but I get that she's trying to be extra friendly.

"I want you to feel like this house is your house, Lily," she says. "Help yourself to anything. By the way, I've moved some things around." She goes on explaining new places to find this or that, the new baking supplies, and a bunch of other stuff.

Just like always, everything in the fridge looks extremely healthy. During the summer, I had trouble finding the basics like chips and guacamole or microwave popcorn. Basically, everything is super good for you, and not very rewarding, unless maybe you're a guinea pig. Since Mom's gone back to school, everything is at our place is, well, easy and fun. Lunch meat. Burritos that you can heat in the microwave. Already-prepared salads.

After we're done chatting about dinner, I excuse myself to get unpacked. I stroll back into the living room and then walk down the hallway.

"I'm happy to help you set up," she says, following me. "I love that kind of thing."

"Thanks," I say, "but I'm good," and head into my room. Well, the guest room that is now my room. I peer around in confusion. My suitcases aren't there, which seems odd. My dad's camera equipment litters the floor. Various high school sports posters line the walls. A couple of monitors sit on a desk crowded with folders.

"Where's my stuff?" I ask, truly baffled.

Kimberly glances at me, a horrified look on her face. "Oh, gosh. Brad forgot to tell you." Brad is my dad's name. It's weird when she calls him that, as though he's a neighbor and not my dad. "I'm sorry, but with the video business sort of exploding, he's taken over the spare bedroom as his office."

My heart sinks. This is only a small three-bedroom townhouse. "But this is where I've always stayed," I say in a small voice.

"That's typical. My absentminded husband forgot to tell you," she says, sighing.

Her husband? How about my dad? But I know she doesn't mean to sound possessive.

Or does she?

No, she's smiling and bought me those blueberries and baking supplies. I think she's really trying to be nice.

"So guess what?" continues Kimberly. "You and Hannah get to share a room. When I was your age, I wanted to share a room with my sister." She claps her hands together like I've just won a prize. "You girls are going to have soooo much fun."

Share a room? Is this some sort of joke?

I have never shared a room with anyone! It's one of the few perks of being an only child. My room is pretty much my sanctuary. I've spent a lot of time decorating my room back at Mom's. I replaced the closet door with a canary-yellow curtain. I painted the walls creamy beige. Keisha jokingly calls it The Spa because I like to play binaural beats, this relaxing music I found on YouTube, and scented candles—lemon and lavender—decorate my dresser. I don't actually light them, though, because Mom's paranoid I might forget to blow them out, but they give it a very relaxed feel.

If I'm going to be abandoned by my mom and forced to live for an entire year with my dad and a stepfamily, at the very least I should have my own space. A surge of anger and disappointment swells. I feel light-headed.

"Does Hannah know?" I ask. "About sharing?"

"Oh yes, she's really looking forward to it." Kimberly's lips tug into a forced smile.

I try to talk myself into this. I imagine what my mom or Keisha might say. *A sister! You can stay up late*

*reading each other's palms. Swap stories. Give advice. Do
each other's hair. Trade clothes.*

Kimberly opens the door, and I look inside.

I can't believe what I see.

Chapter Four
GETTING MESSY

Twin beds flank each other. The far side of the room appears tidy and almost vacant, except for the suitcases standing next to a dresser. Those happen to be my suitcases, so this is obviously my side of the room.

The other side is a complete wreck.

Heaps of clothes litter Hannah's twin bed, which is closest to the door. Shoes, socks, and paper lay strewn on the rug. On a nightstand, stacks of comic books look ready to topple over. Piles of junk cover the dresser—water bottles, wads of gum, retainers, sunglasses, colored pencils, Scotch tape, and mismatched earrings. Swim team trophies and blue ribbons. Oh, and a glass jar labeled GeekGirlCon is stuffed with coins and dollar bills.

Kimberly winces as she also takes in the scary sight. "I told Hannah to clean up her side of the room. I'm so sorry, Lily."

"It's okay." But it's not. It's horrible! Honestly, it's the messiest room I've *ever* seen in my entire life.

Worse than Keisha's older sister, who grows mold for fun on stale pieces of bread so she can post about them on her science blog. Worse than Mom's room after she has pulled an all-nighter studying for an exam and fallen asleep with a pizza box on her bed.

This is my bedroom for the next year? Ugh! Can you call 911 for help with messes?

"It didn't look like this over the summer," I say, trying to keep the frustration out of my voice. Of course, Hannah didn't live here during the summer.

Kimberly takes a step into the room and kicks a few cardboard boxes to create a pathway.

Outside, a car pulls up and doors slam. A few minutes later, Hannah, dressed in gray swim team sweats, waltzes into the bedroom. Tossing her gym bag into the closet, her eyes lift in surprise. "I didn't know Lily would already be here," she says in an almost disinterested voice.

What?! How can she possibly be surprised?

"Hannah," says Kimberly, clearly exasperated. "I told you to clean up. You promised."

"Mom, I had to go to practice."

"Yes, but I told you about it yesterday *and* this morning."

Hannah shrugs as she pulls the plastic slides off her feet. "I had summer reading to finish for language arts."

Why would you wait until the weekend before school starts to do summer reading? Waiting until the last second would give me a heart attack.

"Hannah, you know it's possible," says Kimberly, "to do both your summer reading and clean your room. When Lily was here during the summer, I don't ever recall seeing a single item of clothing on the floor." She shakes her head. "It's your choice to live this way. But it's not fair to Lily."

Hannah glares at me as if my neatness is simply a way of making her look bad. I want to yell at her to grow up, but I contain myself.

"It's okay," I say, trying to be diplomatic. "I have my side of the room."

"Well, I'll let you girls work it out then," says Kimberly, who seems all too eager to close the door behind her.

Desperate to get past the tension, I try to come up with something to break the ice, which is honestly more like a glacier. "So did you do all of those drawings?" I nod at the sketches of elves, goblins, and fairies hanging on her side of the room.

"Yup," Hannah says, glumly. Plopping down onto her bed, she pulls her pink-dotted ponytail holder out of her purple-streaked hair, which goes along with her artsy style. Of course, that doesn't exactly go along with the swimmer vibe. Hannah is . . . interesting, just like Keisha had said.

An elf warrior princess poster hangs above her bed. The elf is big eared but also pretty in an unexpected way. Sort of like Hannah, who's probably one of the tallest girls in her grade and has striking green eyes with long lashes.

"So, um, that poster's intriguing," I say.

"Yeah, it's one of my faves."

"What's GeekGirlCon?" I ask, gesturing at the glass jar filled with money.

"Only the most awesome gaming and comic convention ever. I'm saving up to go."

"Wow, that's cool." I really want to ask her when she plans on cleaning up, if ever, but I hold my tongue.

Yanking a comb through her hair, Hannah winces. "I've got to detangle. It's what happens after swimming."

"Oh, sure. Detangle away."

Silently, I put my stuff away into the empty dresser and set my lemon and lavender candles on top. "Do you mind if I play some relaxing music. Binaural beats?"

"Yes."

Yikes. Guess relaxing is not her thing. After a few minutes, Hannah leans back in her bed and draws in a sketchbook.

As I hang up my clothes on my side of the closet, it's obvious I won't have enough room for all of them. Although Hannah—or most likely Kimberly—pushed her stuff to one side, I only have a third as much space as she does. Her clothes are packed together in no apparent order. How does she find anything?

Peering over her sketch pad, Hannah studies me and then goes back to drawing—er, actually, she goes back to erasing manically.

"Looks like you're having fun there," I say in yet another lame attempt at conversation.

Hannah grips her eraser, scrunching her face. "Erase like a wimp, and you'll still see the ghost of your mess-up lines taunting you, *'Ha, ha! I'm still here. You suck!'* Erase like a piranha, and you'll create a black hole."

"Wow. Okay."

"Ha! Not really. But you do get a really nasty hole in the middle of a panel you've worked on for eons, which means you have to start all over again. Which would be sad. So I start over a lot." Now Hannah seems friendly. Maybe she just needed to relax after swim practice before wanting to talk?

I glance at the crumpled-up sheets of paper circling her bed. "Are those your mess-ups on the floor?"

"Yup." She sounds agitated.

I glance at her blue ribbons. "Are those for art?"

"Yes, the Fall Festival. I won two years in a row. And I'm planning on winning again this year."

Wow. Someone's got an attitude. But a little part of

me admires her confidence. I could never talk like that.

As I continue putting away my clothes, Hannah says, "I used to have enough space in the closet for my art supplies. Now I have to store them down in the basement."

"I'm sorry." Where was I supposed to put my things? "I almost forgot about the basement. Hardly anyone I know has one."

"Yeah, well, this townhouse is ancient. It's from before the 1920s. So now, whenever I need supplies, I have to go all the way down there." She wrinkles her nose in distaste.

"It's not like I asked to move into this junk pile."

Oh no, I shouldn't have said that. I went too far. But clearly I couldn't hold it in or I would have.

I pull my gaze from her piles of messes and notice Hannah's bottom lip does this trembly thing.

She scrambles off her bed and rushes out of the room before I can apologize.

Well, if I'm honest, I don't really want to apologize. After all, she was the one who brought this on.

I just have to remember to keep my mouth shut for the rest of the year if I'm going to get along with Hannah like I promised Mom.

That evening, Maisie nips me as I step out of the bathroom right before dinner. Kimberly says it's because I was wearing a baseball hat, and that Maisie is afraid of hats. Luckily, the skin doesn't break. Kimberly banishes Maisie to the backyard, and Dad says Maisie can't sleep in the room with us, which is fine with me, because I don't think I'd want Maisie to sleep in my bed.

Outside the sliding glass door to the kitchen, Maisie yips and taps on the glass with her paw. Poor puppy! She looks so sad being left out all alone in the backyard. I suddenly feel desperate to video chat Mom, but I know that she's not even in Morocco yet, since the whole trip will take almost sixteen hours with a layover in Paris. Right before she took off I did get a couple of texts from her showing off her window view from the plane.

While we get ready for bed, Maisie whimpers on the other side of the bedroom door to be let in. Hannah tells me that she won't be able to sleep without Maisie in the room. And because of that, she's going to look like a zombie for the first day of school on Tuesday. How can Hannah already need her dog to go to bed? They just adopted Maisie. I wonder how Hannah was falling sleep before.

"I hope you like nineties grunge because it's what I wake up to," she tells me as I continue to contemplate her nighttime habits.

"Um, I think, maybe, my dad used to listen to it. I'm more into pop."

"I hate pop. It's such a sellout." She points at her phone. "FYI. I snooze twice." She points to the window. "I always sleep with it open."

"Even when it's rainy?"

"Yup. I'm a fresh-air girl. Otherwise, I get too hot." I see that she's wearing long-sleeve pajamas so this makes no sense.

"Maybe just wear a t-shirt to bed?"

"Bad idea."

"Well, good night then." It's definitely not.

She doesn't say anything back.

When the lights are out, I dive into my thoughts and the first thing that comes to mind is: I can't believe how unfriendly Hannah's being. In the past, she's basically semi-ignored me, but now she seems hostile. She obviously is as thrilled to share a room, and possibly a home, as I am.

The pillow is too foamy and hard. I try to mash my head down, but it's like there's a spring under it.

I try to lie on my right side.

My left.

The bed's too cold. The room is too unfamiliar and Hannah is already asleep and softly snoring. Without Maisie.

It's going to be a long night.

A long year.

Chapter Five
A GOOD GHOULISH PLAN

On Tuesday morning of the first day of school, I read the first part of a text from Mom. She says it was past midnight Tacoma time when she arrived and morning in Morocco. We had decided that we would video chat on the weekends at noon my time—and eight at night for her—since when I get home from school, she would be asleep. On certain weekdays, if I was willing to wake up early, we could video chat. I read the rest of the text:

I'm sooo tired and jetlagged. I fell asleep standing up in the customs line in the airport. When the plane landed in Rabat, the light was so golden. From what I see, Morocco is beautiful. Can't wait to explore! Miss you, babu! Xoxoxo

Babu is my nickname that only Mom uses. Even though it's dorky, it makes my heart lift.

At first when I text Mom back, I start to tell her about Hannah's hostile attitude, and how the room is a hazard zone, but I realize that would show her that I'm starting out in critical mode. So I erase it all. Instead, I try to put a positive spin on everything:

Maisie is soooo cute but a rascal. When Kimberly was making dinner, she just had sad puppy eyes and begged for people food.

Hannah and I are sharing a room, which means we'll get to know each other super well.

I love you and miss you!

I spring out of bed and hurry to the bathroom to take my shower. I'm happily imagining the feel of warm water spraying over my face when someone whizzes past me in the hall.

Hannah! The bathroom door slams in front of my nose. Seconds later, water spurts out of the shower.

I have no choice but to wait for my turn. I wait. And wait.

Back in the bedroom, I text Keisha: *Hannah beat me to the shower :(.*

Keisha texts back, *Welcome to my world!* Keisha's older sister, Alexis, is famous for long showers. And singing off-key. *Tell Hannah to hurry,* adds Keisha,

I don't want to be rude, I type back. Instead, I pick out three different outfits and ask Keisha to get her thoughts. We always coordinate what we're wearing on the first day of school, since we don't want to be too matchy-matchy. Or too different either.

She tells me to go for the jeans with the peasant blouse because it looks pirate-y.

I heard that Ethan is really into pirate movies, she texts.

Maybe I should wear an eye patch. Ha ha, I text back, and then check out the time. Yikes! We need to leave in twenty-five minutes to make the bus. Pacing in the room, I practically trip over Hannah's clogs. I toss them into the jumbled side of the closet, where they land with a clatter. Is that hard to put away your shoes? It's the first day of school. Of all days, I want to feel calm.

Right now I'm definitely not.

When the shower *finally* stops, Hannah doesn't come out.

"Can you hurry up in there?" I plead, banging on the door.

"Stop!" snaps Hannah. "You're going to break it."

Does she think I'm Wonder Woman? I wish, because then I'd take my invisible jet and fly to be with Mom.

Hannah steps into the hallway with a towel wrapped around her middle. "You better hurry up, Lily."

"*I* better hurry up? You took forever."

"Then get up earlier."

Kimberly pads down the hallway towards us. She looks great in a crisp gray skirt and short, green sweater top that contrasts nicely with her red hair. "Morning, girls. Breakfast is waiting for you in the kitchen."

"Thanks, Mom," Hannah says in the sweetest voice ever. "I'm ready." She turns to me and purrs, "You can use my conditioner. And my shampoo. It says it's for color-treated hair. But it doesn't have to be."

"Oh, thanks," I say, even though I don't feel thankful. I'm going to have time for a three-minute shower and nothing else.

I remind myself the way in which I want to live—if you don't have anything nice to say, *don't say it at all*.

Plus, if I snap at Hannah now, it will just make me look bad in front of Kimberly since Hannah is acting so thoughtful.

As I hurry into the bathroom, my frustration cools just a little.

When I turn on the spigot, I lift up my face, ready for a lovely—though quick—warm shower.

The water is freezing! I shriek and hop in and out of the icy spray, gritting my teeth, ready to kill Hannah. It's so cold, I expect the water to turn into sleet. She did this on purpose.

As I towel off, my teeth chatter. When I open the door, Maisie barks. "What's going on with her?" I ask, ready to lose it.

"Take the towel off your head," says Hannah, who's standing in the hallway and admiring herself in the mirror as she combs her hair. "Maisie doesn't like it when people have anything on their heads. That includes towels."

Maisie woofs so loudly I expect the walls to vibrate.

"Are you serious?" I pull off my towel, and Maisie quiets down.

"Enjoy the shower?" asks Hannah coyly.

"There was no hot water," I say slowly so I don't erupt.

"Wow. Sorry. Maybe my mom started the washer or something."

Or something. I get dressed in record time.

"Better eat!" Kimberly calls out.

Hannah and I speed into the kitchen. "Need to power up for your IMs today, Hannah," says Kimberly.

IMs? I'm guessing it's something swim team-ish.

Dad has made scrambled eggs and French toast for breakfast. "I thought it'd be good to start your first day right," he says, smiling at me.

"Thanks," I say.

"Is anything wrong?" asks Kimberly.

"First day of school nerves?" says Dad.

"That's it." I grit my teeth, then try to relax. Maybe Hannah just lost track of the time and honestly forgot all about me during her hot-water spa-treatment moment. Maybe it wasn't on purpose.

Doubtful.

At school, as I stroll down the hall to morning advisory, all of the bad Hannah things are canceled out. Because walking right in front of me is none other than Ethan Sanarov.

Yes, *that* Ethan. Not only is he supposed to be a

good swimmer, but he has own his YouTube channel with two hundred subscribers. Not a huge number, but a lot for our middle school.

The back of his shiny blond hair touches the tip of his collar. I'm so close behind him that my nose is practically in his sweater.

I never thought that a sweater could be this interesting. But it is because Ethan is inside of it. I had planned on running into the girls' restroom, but no way am I doing that now.

New item on my to-do list in my weekly planner: sticking as close to Ethan as peanut butter on jelly.

The hallways are crowded. For once, I'm thrilled about it because I can easily eavesdrop on Ethan without looking too obvious. He's saying something to his friend Josh Washington about signing up for the Fall Festival Haunted House committee.

"Really?" says Josh as they navigate around a clump of lost-looking sixth graders. "Dude, I'm signing up to sell tickets. It's seriously the easiest job. You just show up that day. No committee meetings."

"Boring," says Ethan, pushing up his glasses, which I think make him look so smart. "Dude, on the Haunted House committee, you can take care of the school volunteering requirement by scaring little kids."

"Just looking at you would do that," says Josh.

Ethan playfully shoves him.

Then the warning bell rings and everyone rushes to advisory.

Except for me, that is. I'm so happy I practically float. Now I know how I will get my required school volunteer hours—working on the Haunted House committee! Oh, it's awesome being a seventh grader and knowing exactly what to do and where to go. Just one year ago, I remember being in a panic that I'd be late to every class because I had no idea where I was going.

When I stroll into advisory, Keisha hugs me and we twirl together. Well, Keisha twirls and I pretend to twirl. That's because she's a competitive ice-skater and actually knows what she's doing.

"So you look happy," she notes after we are done spinning.

"Oh yeeeeees!" I say with a huge grin in my face. "I have news!"

"Tell me."

"In a second. I need to go to the bathroom before the bell rings." I didn't go earlier because of my up-close-and-almost-personal Ethan sighting. And now I really need to!

"You're cruel," says Keisha.

"I know." I zip to the restroom which luckily is right across the hallway.

When I return, someone's in my seat.

And that someone happens to be none other than Reese Pham, the boy who has teased me the most since kindergarten. He's on the short side and wears this black beanie and old vintage jacket with patches on the sleeves because he thinks it looks cool. He and his group of friends are known as the Sharpie Boys because they always carry their skateboards in their backpacks along with Sharpies they use to write on each other's bags. I once saw Reese scrawl **YOU'RE UGLY** on his friend Jonah Schlesinger's lunch bag. So wrong. The Sharpie Boys joke around all the time and are never serious.

Oh, and a lot of girls somehow think Reese is really cute. Because of his dimples, I guess. And his green eyes (his Dad is Vietnamese and his mom is from Sweden). And swoopy black hair. And he uses his looks and jokey attitude to get what he wants, which is mostly to get out of doing things, which is annoying, so I don't see cuteness. I see a pest!

"Excuse me," I say to Reese, "But I'm sitting here." Somehow when it comes to Reese, I don't have a problem letting him know how I feel.

"Not according to the seating chart, Magic," he says. Magic is his nickname for me, and I have no idea why. It's one of those unsolved mysteries. I once asked him about it, and he told me that when the time was right, he'd tell me.

Which was weird and annoying and *so* Reese.

"Are you sure you graduated to the seventh grade?" asks Keisha.

"Ha ha. I'm not joking about the seating chart," says Reese. "It's a new seventh-grade thing, Magic. Mr. Pastcan has it." With a serious expression, he gestures to our advisory teacher, who is busy counting out stacks of paper at his desk. Mr. Pastcan is wearing a bow tie. It's not a first day of school thing—he's known for them.

"I didn't hear him announce that," Keisha points out logically.

"Go up and ask him," urges Reese. "You both should."

Keisha's eyebrows scrunch, and I'm sure I look equally confused.

Together, we stroll up to Mr. Pastcan and ask about the seating chart. Of course, it's a scam. By the time we get back, Reese's friend, Jonah, is cracking up and sitting in Keisha's seat.

"We're telling Mr. Pastcan," states Keisha, her face puckering in irritation.

I shake my head and whisper, "No, don't. Then Reese will know how much he gets to me."

Grabbing Keisha's hand, I pull her to the back of the class and find two empty desks. "Really? Reese and Jonah have to be in our advisory?" I set my backpack down onto the floor.

"God's punishing us," says Keisha. "We must have done something really wrong."

"Maybe." But I haven't done anything wrong. That would be Hannah.

"Those two are never serious. Even for one second."

"Maybe when they sleep," I joke and Keisha snorts.

While Mr. Pastcan takes roll and then hands out a bunch of forms for us to give our parents, Keisha says, "You better tell your news or else you'll be sorry."

"What news?" says Reese, who just happens to be throwing away a tissue in the trash can near my desk.

"You are such a busybody," scolds Keisha.

"Inquiring minds want to know." Reese grins.

"Oh, shut up," I say, and Reese thankfully walks back to his seat.

Leaning over, I whisper to Keisha and tell her about my Ethan sighting. She tells me that she thinks it's a sign. Keisha is really into signs and good luck. For example, she always wears the same necklace—a silver musical note—whenever she has a competition. I ask her about ice-skating, and she fills me in on her latest tricks, as well as gives me an update on Quinn, her crush who also trains at the same rink but goes to a different middle school. When Keisha asks about Hannah, my stomach tenses.

"Did she at least clean up her side of the room?" Keisha holds up her thumb and pointer finger. "Just a teensy bit?"

"Nope. Her clothes and comic books have officially invaded."

"Get a measuring tape and throw up a divider. You have to tell her it's wrong,"

I roll my eyes. "Like that would stop her."

"Talk to your dad. Let him know how you feel. And tell him to move his stuff out of the office so you can have it back as a bedroom."

"I can't. Filming high school sports has turned into a real thing. He needs to store his equipment there."

"Well, that's good." Keisha knows all about my dad's previous not-very-successful business ideas. For example, a tea shop, Tearrific. Apparently, nobody wanted tea in the city of Tacoma, just coffee. And he also fixed up a van and traveled to people's houses to mount and frame artwork and photos. The business was called Frame-it-Up. Only the cost of the van and the gas was more than he'd charge for his services.

"While I'm happy that his video production company is doing well, sharing a room sucks!"

Mr. Pastcan stares at me. "Watch your language," he admonishes.

My face warms and Reese smirks.

"Don't worry," whispers Keisha. "Things will get better."

I'm thinking how much I doubt that's true when Mr. Pastcan says he needs to go over some announcements, including the Fall Festival. Oh yeah—I'm definitely volunteering for that! And I'm going to enter my apple pie recipe for the contest part of it, too!

Mr. Pastcan hands out sheets of paper on which we can rank the committees we'd like to work on.

"I'm putting down the Haunted House commit-tee," I whisper to Keisha, who gives me a thumbs-up. She signs up for Refreshments.

"Seventh grade is going to be good," she says.

"Yes, it's going to be so awesome!" At least I hope so. But with Hannah around, I'm not so sure.

Chapter Six
CLASSIFIED INFORMATION

After school, Keisha and I walk home together. Okay, it's weird to call the townhouse my actual home. But I guess it is, for now. We decide to go on foot instead of taking the bus in order to get a little extra exercise, not that Keisha needs it because of ice-skating. It's more that Keisha has a day off from practice, and it seemed like a fun thing to do.

It's surprisingly hot for September, so we have to stop to take a swig of water from our bottles in front of the townhouse. It's on a busy street. Nothing like my old house before the divorce. That was a split-level set off from the road, and, in front, was a grove of old oaks. When I was little, I thought it was a real forest and would pretend that I was lost and make small forts out of fallen branches and leaves. In the backyard, we had a flat lawn with cherry and plum trees. My mom and I would pick the fruit to make our cobblers.

Hannah isn't home because she's at some theater class, and Kimberly greets us at the door. She offers to make us root beer floats, which surprises me since she usually doesn't stock up on unhealthy things. Then she runs out because she and my dad have some appointments with a realtor to look at houses.

"I had no idea you guys were moving," Keisha says.

"Yeah, apparently. They explained everything last night during dinner. This place is too small. Especially if me and you-know-who have to share a room."

"Is it really that bad?"

I pull Keisha down the hallway and we peek into the room. She clamps a hand over her mouth. "It's that bad. Like there was an earthquake on Hannah's side."

"I was going to say nuclear explosion. But, yeah. Definitely disaster-ish."

Back in the kitchen, we sip the root beer floats at the table and Keisha loves on Maisie.

"She's so cute," she says, petting her. Maisie's tail thumps furiously and she licks both of our hands.

"She is, but if you wear a hat, she goes crazy, so watch out."

"Got it."

"Just make sure to warn me if you hear Hannah. She's not supposed to come back for another hour." I'm basing this on what I know about her schedule, anyway. Keisha and I talk about her ice-skating, my flute playing, our teachers, and our crushes.

"Ethan's gotten cuter this year, if it's even possible," I say. "Plus, taller. I can't believe I'm going to be on the same committee with him."

"Maybe you'll actually be able to talk to him in person."

"Yeah." I say, sighing. "And even work together."

A door slams.

I glance up. Hannah stands in the entranceway to the townhouse. How had I not heard the door open? She must be back from either swim practice or her theater class. It's hard to keep track. I peer at Keisha and she looks at me in terror. I know we are both thinking the same thing. Did she hear? Does she now know I like Ethan?

This could be bad.

Hannah says hi and then zips into her room. Excuse me. *Our* room.

"Do you think she heard?" I whisper.

"Does it matter?"

"They're in the same grade. And on the swim team together."

"Yeah, but it's not like they're good friends."

"Right. Probably not."

After Keisha leaves, I practice the flute, watch a pie baking video, and look up a blog about dog training. Maybe they have tips on how to train Maisie. Sitting in bed, I read a text from Mom. She tells me about visiting this huge tomb of the king's grandfather, which seems like a potentially scary place to visit. But maybe it's a thing.

The sea air, the silence make this spot mystical and beautiful. And I realized that sometimes we just need to appreciate the moment.

Wow, I guess it wasn't Halloween creepy. I write Mom back and tell her about the first day of school. How I might make first chair this year in band and a little about Keisha's new skating routine. Then I think about appreciating what's right in front of me. That would be Hannah, unfortunately. She's leaning back against cushions on her bed and sketching on her iPad.

"What are you doing?" I ask, genuinely curious.

"Drawing."

Okay, this one's on me. I just asked the most Captain Obvious question ever invented on the planet. "I know. But what?"

I hop over a bunch of junk to get to Hannah's side of the room. She shows me her iPad. It's some sort of piece of fruit, I think. "What do you think?" She squints, her eyes challenging me. If I say it looks like a watermelon and it's supposed to be cantaloupe, will she cry?

I try to be diplomatic. "I'm not really sure."

"It's the curve of a flower petal." Her voice is annoyed.

"Oh, I see." I'm afraid to ask any other questions, but I can't help myself. "Earlier when you first came back from your class, did you hear Keisha and me talking?"

Without answering, Hannah jumps out of bed and deposits money from her wallet into her GeekGirlCon jar. Maybe it's her allowance money?

"Did you sign up for any Fall Festival committees?" I ask.

"Yes," says Hannah. "The Craft committee."

"I'm doing Haunted House."

Hannah frowns. "Really? Every year the haunted house is always so lame."

"Maybe I can improve it."

"Good luck with that." That's when Maisie bounds up to me and stands on her hind legs. Her nails dig into my chest.

"Down, Maisie." I nudge her with my knee. "She needs to learn some manners."

"It's not her fault." Hannah then tells me about adopting Maisie from a doodle rescue organization she had found on the web. How she and her mom visited Maisie for the first time at the home of a foster family who took in abandoned goldendoodles. Suddenly, for the first time, I'm relating to Maisie. And seeing a softer side of Hannah. At least, a little softer.

Then, out of the blue, Hannah glares at the walls above my bed and dresser. "Why haven't you put anything up?" she says in an accusatory way.

"Well, my candles are out," I say defensively. "I guess I haven't had time. I like to think about the look

I'm going for. Not just throw something up." I peer at Hannah's posters, which have been haphazardly scotch-taped to the walls.

"Maybe there's a photo of a certain boy you'd like to hang up on the wall." She's smirking.

"No," I lie. But inside I'm thinking, *Oh no. Hannah knows about Ethan. She sees him every day.*

This is the opposite of good.

My stomach curls into a knot.

Crush info is classified, and I think it's just landed in the wrong hands.

chapter seven
QUESTIONS AND ANSWERS

Before school on Wednesday, I get up early to video chat with Mom. It's 6:00 a.m. when I settle into the living room couch. Everyone is asleep, even Maisie.

On the screen of my phone, Mom stands in a courtyard, decorated with colorful tiles. She's right outside of work and, luckily, the Wi-Fi is strong. She tells me about her awesome new apartment. How even though it's small, it's filled with light. And that everyone at work is super friendly.

"So how are you?" she asks, and she's so cheerful that I don't really want to tell her. And anyway, what would I say? Hannah takes long showers on purpose? She's not neat. She's rude.

"C'mon, honey. I want to hear what's going on with you."

"Just school stuff." I tell her about how I signed up for the Haunted House committee and that the first meeting is this afternoon. I also tell her about my plans for baking the perfect apple pie for the festival contest.

"Maybe you could practice and I could watch you bake."

"That's such a great idea, Mom." Then Maisie wakes up and bounds over to me, her tail swishing. She jumps up and I have to knee her down.

"She's soo cute," coos Mom. "And eager."

"A little too eager." I pet Maisie behind her ears. "And she doesn't like hats or towels on your head."

"She sounds like a bit of a handful."

"Yeah, luckily she's sweet."

"She'll calm down as she gets older."

"I don't think I can wait that long. I've got to do something about it. I've been looking at videos."

"I'm sure you could train her," says Mom.

After we hang up, I think about how teaching Maisie a thing or two is a good idea. I'd really work on starting to train her.

By the time morning advisory on Wednesday arrives, I'm feeling excited by my new sense of purpose. I am totally going to figure out how to teach Maisie to behave better. And maybe we'll even work on some new tricks. Add that to my planning the perfect pie, practicing the flute, and being part of the Haunted House committee, and my life is going to be nice and full.

The rest of day, I'm floating through school, thinking about the Haunted House committee. Specifically thinking about being on the committee with Ethan.

I float through social studies, band, lunch, gym, and pre-algebra. At one point, Hannah passes by Keisha and me during fifth-period break, and we wave. Wow. We're so different, it's almost comical. Today, her purple-streaked hair is all loose and a little wild-looking. My hair, on the other hand, is pulled back in a neat ponytail. Hannah's also wearing bright pink high-tops with black jeans and a plaid lumberjack shirt that's two sizes too big. And, hold up—she's wearing my t-shirt underneath it!

Hey, that's my shirt! I want to scream.

It's my hole-infested tie-dyed one. The one I made with my mom during Family Day at camp. It's too big for me, since I'm on the little side, but it's just the right size for Hannah.

But I'm not going yell. And I'm not going to let Hannah pop my happy bubble.

Plus, today, she's been weirdly friendly. Maybe her moodiness has gone away? I try my hardest not to be mad about the shirt. After all, it's just a shirt, and Hannah is smiling and even skipping down the hall.

The Haunted House committee meets in the magazine area of the library with Ms. Petrie, an eighth-grade language arts teacher in charge of the Fall Festival. The committee sits around a bunch of round tables. Other groups meet in the Maker Space, near the circulation desk, the beanbag chair area in the stacks, and in the computer room.

Eighth graders, including Lindsay and Thanh Ha, who are known for being really good students, are seated at one of the Haunted House committee tables. There's also a boy wearing a baseball cap sitting with them—Ethan. His cute wire-rimmed glasses make him look like Clark Kent. Like he doesn't want other people to know just how cute he is. And plus, they make him look very mature.

There's an extra chair right next to him.

A little voice tells me to go for it. It's Keisha's voice. And it's saying what her coach tells her after she's trained and ready for a new trick: *Push away fear. You can do this, Lily.*

I stroll over, trying to look casual, and take the chair next to Ethan. My heart pounds in my ears.

"Hey," he says.

"Hi," I manage. I can't think of what to say next. My brain is like frozen slush.

"Aren't you Hannah's sister?" His eyes are so alert and intelligent. I feel like I could study them for a long time.

"Yes," I say, suddenly remembering how to talk. "Stepsister, actually."

"Cool." Cool because he thinks Hannah is cool? Or cool because I'm cool?

Does it matter? We have spoken! Actual words have been exchanged.

Then there's a tap on my shoulder. "This is my seat." I glance up. It's Hannah, her lips curled into a sneer.

"What are you doing here?" I squeak.

"The same thing you are."

Hannah is on the Haunted House committee? No. No! She couldn't have signed up for the very same committee as me. What about the Craft committee? Or the Be Mean and Annoying committee?

"Your stuff isn't here," I say this in a calm voice but I really want to scream it.

"It is now." Hannah drops her backpack so it lands with a thud on my feet.

I press my lips together to keep from yelping. Leaning over, I whisper in her ear. "We need to talk."

She definitely changed groups after she overheard me babble on about my crush.

Hannah grimaces. "If you have something to say, Lily, say it to everyone. Whispering is rude."

What?! There's no way I'm going to talk to her, really talk to her, in front of cool eighth-grade girls like Lindsay and Thanh Ha and *definitely* not in front of Ethan.

Hannah smiles. It's like she knows she has me.

I scurry away from the table so Ethan doesn't see my cheeks flame.

Then I think a happy thought: Ethan didn't tell me not to sit down. He didn't say, *I'm reserving that chair for Hannah*. Maybe I intrigue him? Maybe he wanted me to sit there. My heart flutters.

I sneak a glance before figuring out where else to sit.

One table is full of sixth-grade boys. I only know one of their names, a tall boy named Samir who used to be in my tae kwon do class. The guys are on their phones playing some sort of game that's popular right now that I definitely don't like. I'm not about to sit with sixth graders anyway, so I sit at a table by myself. And then I immediately regret it. I'm probably looking like a loser right about now.

I sneak one more glance at Ethan to see if he's noticing that I'm sitting all alone. He's talking to Hannah. Ugh. I'm sure she started the conversation just to torture me.

Well, it's working. I never understood what people meant when they said that their blood boiled. But now I do.

I stare down at the table, contemplating how pathetic I must look to Ethan. The girl sitting by herself. Suddenly, I hear chairs scuffling and I look up. It's Reese and his friends. I've been invaded.

"Seriously?" I say. "You guys are on the Haunted House committee, too?"

"Watch out. The party has started," says Reese. Today, he's wearing a t-shirt that says, *I'm a Palindrome—Tacocat.*

His friend Jonah beats on the table like a drummer. "Oh yeah!"

"Ignore them," says Luke, who's the only member of the Sharpies to be a little more mature. He's blond with a cowlick that always looks freshly popped up.

"Don't worry. I will."

Keisha's mom always likes to say: Be careful what you wish for because it might come true. And I immediately know that I've brought this upon myself. I wanted not to be alone. And now Reese and the Sharpie Boys are with me.

Reese is a complete contrast to Ethan, who is so mature. He's actually brought a book with him. The title is *How to be a YouTube Star.*

"Okay, it's time to get started," Ms. Petrie tells our group. "Other than today, we're going to meet on Mondays. I just wanted you all to get a chance to know each other. So please say hi to your fellow ghoul friends."

We half wave, and the Sharpie Boys boo at each other, which the sixth graders think is hysterical. And okay, the way they do it is kind funny. The eighth-grade table seems like they already know each other really well.

"So, in advance of this meeting, Hannah Dietz let me know that she was willing to chair the committee. Hannah's an eighth grader, and an accomplished artist, who has won our Fall Festival art contest each year starting when she was a sixth grader."

Hannah smiles as the kids at her table high-five her, including Ethan.

Wait. Hannah is going to be the chair? This is a nightmare. I know that as a Haunted House member we are supposed to create nightmares, but this is far too realistic.

"I'm going to let Hannah take charge," says Ms. Petrie. "But I'm here to support you and give advice."

She's going to let Hannah actually be in charge?

My ears buzz and I can't focus on the rest of what Ms. Petrie is saying. Something about how she'll be running back and forth between committees and then about rules.

My eyes flick over to Hannah, who is positively beaming. Her face is so lit up, she could be a lighthouse. No, that's wrong. Lighthouses save people and prevent wrecks.

Hannah is a wreck.

"There's to be no running in the library," Ms. Petrie says. She looks over at the sixth graders and then over at my table, as if we were about to shoot out of a starting gate at any moment. "And number two, there's no food or drinks in the library."

"But what if we're hungry?" says a sixth grader.

"You're welcome to give yourself a snack break," says Ms. Petrie. "Also, if you'd like to meet outside of school at people's houses, you're welcome to do that as well." She glances at my stepsister in an admiring kind of way. "Okay, Hannah, why don't you take it from here?"

Hannah struts up and stands next to Ms. Petrie. "I'm leaving you all in *very* good hands."

Apparently, Ms. Petrie doesn't know my stepsister very well.

Hannah tucks her hair behind her ears. "This is going to be a lot of work. But hey! It's also going to rock. Last year, the Haunted House was definitely not scary." She pauses and rolls her eyes. They had bobbing for apples and someone actually had the audacity to have a Casper the Friendly Ghost costume." She makes quotes in the air. "With an emphasis on 'friendly.'"

"Boo! Anything friendly," says Reese.

"Exactly," says Thanh Ha. "We need to be creepy."

"And weird," says Lindsay.

"Yes, definitely scary," continues Hannah. "I was thinking we could do montages from scary movies. I love love love horror films by the way, but don't let me"—she taps her chest—"sway you."

Hannah likes scary movies? I do, too. Although maybe not the kind you're thinking about. I like old-fashioned horror movies from a real long time ago. I watch them with my grandma who lives back in Philadelphia. She's into this classic movie channel, plus this old-timey horror movie channel. With her, I've watched *Swamp Thing*, *Jaws*, and *Bride of Frankenstein*. I can't believe that Hannah and I have anything in common.

"There's a sign-in sheet." Hannah holds it up. "This lets *me* know who's actually here so they can get their volunteering credits." You can tell she loves the power.

"So let's everyone talk about ideas for the Haunted House," she continues. "And if you don't think you can handle being here, remember this is volunteering. So if you don't like it, you can leave."

She looks at me, her eyes narrowed.

It feels like a direct challenge.

There is no way I'm leaving.

"I know that, as eighth graders, we're used to a lot of responsibility," she says, glancing at Ethan's table. "We'll be going to high school next year. But for you *younger* kids"—her eyes meet mine—"this is definitely not goof-off time."

Younger kids? It's not like we're a decade apart. Just one year!

"You'll notice in the center of each table, Ms. Petrie has left us a big piece of paper and markers," says Hannah. "Everyone, I want you to discuss your best ideas for the Haunted House. Write them down on the sheets of paper. And then next time we meet, we can vote on what we'd like to actually do."

"How about a roller coaster?" calls out Reese. "In the middle of the Haunted House!"

"We need to be realistic," says Hannah. I look over at the eighth-grade table. Ethan appears to be looking at his phone, probably doing research for amazing Haunted House concepts. "So discuss with your table, and then we'll regroup."

Hannah goes back to her seat, the one right next to Ethan.

I think I'm going to be sick,

Someone, as in Reese, is rudely snapping his fingers in my face. "Hello. Earth to Lily. We are discussing ideas."

"What? Oh. Right. I guess we need to do something scary."

Reese shakes his head. "Scary is overrated. People want funny."

"I know," says Jonah. "Force-feeding someone worms. Only the worms are made out of candy."

"That just sounds mean," I say.

"How about dipping onions in caramel?" says Luke. "And putting them on sticks, so they look like caramel apples."

"Man, that's awesome!" says Reese. "Can you imagine if someone bit into one of those?"

I shake my head. "You go into a haunted house to be scared, not be tricked."

"You go to be surprised," says Reese. "It's the opposite of what anyone would expect."

Luke gives a thumbs-up. "It'd be awesome."

"We could also make a balloon cake," adds Reese. "I did it to my sister. You put icing all over a balloon so it looks like a cake. She freaked!"

The Sharpie Boys go on to discuss other ridiculous pranks while I come up with the idea of science lab. Keisha is really into science and wants to be a doctor when she grows up. Well, after she wins her Olympic medal.

After about fifteen minutes, the whole committee discusses all of the ideas.

Reese lists a series of pranks while I mention the demented science lab. The sixth graders want to do a graveyard scene, an autopsy room, a room full of bad smells, or a zoo for people.

The eighth graders want to do a zombie high school, vampires, a crazy butcher, or a witch's coven.

"These are really good ideas," says Hannah.

Everyone is smiling and looking really proud of themselves. I can't believe she thinks all of the ideas are good. A room full of bad smells? Can't anyone else see through to her fakeness?

I want to yell out, "Faker!" But I don't. I can't.

I wish there was some way that I could get Hannah, some way to put her in her place.

When Ms. Petrie checks back in, Hannah proudly shows her our poster board with ideas. "I love it." She looks at the clock on the wall. "But it's time to go. . . . So you all decided, right? You voted on which ideas you want to get started on? We have a tight timeline."

I notice that Hannah's face reddens. "Um, no," she admits. "We didn't get to that." She definitely should have planned it better, I think.

"So we should probably meet again on Friday," Reese suggests. His friends look at him like he's crazy.

"Do the rest of you think that the committee should meet on Friday afternoon then?" asks Ms. Petrie.

"It's actually a good idea," I say, surprised by Reese sounding so reasonable.

The eighth-grade girls nod. Ethan doesn't say anything; his eyes are glued on his phone.

"So meeting on Friday does sound like a very good idea, Reese," says Ms. Petrie.

Reese gives me a goofy thumbs-up. "In fact, I'm going to have all of the committees meet." The Sharpie Boys groan.

And as soon as Ms. Petrie leaves, the entire committee boos, a legit boo, and the Sharpie Boys toss spitballs at Reese's head and mine.

"Dude, you just signed us up for more work!" Luke shouts.

Reese ducks mostly in time.

I don't. Now my hair is full of spitballs.

"Look like you've been busy getting decorated, Lily," Hannah says loudly.

Ethan stares at me. The Ethan. My Ethan.

And then it comes to me.

Exactly what I need to do. And Reese of all people has supplied me with the answer.

chapter eight
SPITBALLING

I grab Keisha's hand and head toward the bathroom.

"Um, what are we doing?" she asks as we fly through the hallway.

"I'll explain." Together we zip into the girls' restroom. The doors of the girls' and boys' bathrooms are always left open. It has something to do with security and safety.

By the sink, I whip the spitballs out of my hair.

Keisha picks out the remaining ones. "Okay, I get it now. You needed me to help you not look like you have a very bad case of dandruff."

I groan, looking down at the floor. I can't bear to look at myself in the mirror.

"No, it's not that bad."

I keep my eyes on the floor, remembering Ethan seeing me like this. The bathroom tiles are the palest shade of pink. Some of the tiles are missing and have been replaced with orange ones. Orange and pink do not look good together, especially in a bathroom.

Some girl with braids whips out of one of the stalls. With the doors flung open, you can see the toilet seat cover dispenser. A giant one.

Which gives me a giant idea.

As I brush out the last of the confetti, Keisha asks me if I want to come watch her skating practice later this afternoon. "It'll cheer you up. I'm going to be working on this move. I have these new skates, and it's helping me hold the landings."

"That's great. But I can't. I've got to be home for something. Something that requires perfect timing." I watch Keisha's bottom lip drop in disappointment.

"Don't worry. I'll catch you another time," I add as I yank several toilet seat covers out of a dispenser.

"What are you doing?" gasps Keisha.

"Well, first I have to tell you that Ethan spoke to me." I put my hand over my heart. "And he totally knows who I am." Then I tell Keisha how awful Hannah was. Every detail. All the crazy meanness.

"Woo, boy. That's one cranky girl," says Keisha. "She definitely got up on the wrong side of the bed."

"The wrong side of the bed? Cranky? It's far beyond that. It's the reason I can't watch you skate today. Hanging out with Reese and his friends gave me a little idea of what I need to do to get back at Hannah. I can't start an open war with her at home or on my committee. For lots of reasons."

"Because of your Ethan." She trills his name.

"Shhh," I put my fingers to my lips. "E."

"Right, E, then."

"And I'm not going to go around saying mean things about Hannah to anyone. Because I just can't go there. And I'm not going to start a fight with her. I'm not a yeller. Or I refuse to be one because of . . ."

"Your parents."

"Exactly." Keisha knows exactly how I feel about my parents fighting so much right before they split up. She was there for me the whole time, even though we were just in third grade. That's pretty much when we began our tradition of me watching her skate—so I didn't have to be at my house. Watching Keisha dance and jump on the ice rink like a fairy princess was my great escape.

"So I have found a new way to tell Hannah how I feel. A fun way. But an awesome way."

"Toilet paper covers?"

"It's just prank. All in good fun! But I'll make my point. Genius, right?"

"Um, well. I don't know. Why don't you just call her on her stuff? Say how you feel?"

"What I'm going to do is stuff the toilet seat covers into Hannah's binder so when she opens it up—bam! The toilet seat covers will spring right out like a bunch of Slinkies."

"Do you really need to do this?"

"Oh yeah," I say. "I do. She's out to get me." I count all of the horrors on my fingers. "The mess in our room. The shower. Taking over on the Haunted House committee. And then purposely called me out in public, just so Ethan would see me looking like I had Halloween lice in my hair."

"It didn't look like lice."

"It didn't look good."

"Still."

Suddenly, I'm filled with purpose. "I'm not going to let Hannah win. This is happening."

"Really. Maybe you should try to talk to her first."

"I've tried to start conversations. It does. Not. Help." I'm going do things in a way that will work for me. Didn't my mom believe you have to never give up? Never back down?

And that's exactly what I'm about to do.

Chapter Nine
SETUP AND PUNCHLINES

When I get home, my dad and stepmom are out working and Hannah is at her theater class, so the timing is perfect! I swoop into the bedroom and discover Hannah's backpack on her bed.

As I start to stuff her binder with the toilet seat covers, I hear a shuffling sound, and panic. Could Hannah already be home?

A dog nose pokes into the doorway. I laugh. It's only Maisie, who doesn't bark at me. I scratch her chin and her tail thumps wildly.

I've really done the prank!

Even though I'm just a little nervous, I also feel like I've done something! Checking my phone for notifications, I see a new text from Mom. She raves about her new home.

I love Rabat! It's the capital and the perfect size city. My greatest find has been this awesome crêperie. When I get home, the first thing I'm going do is figure out how to make a crepe, and we are going to go crepe crazy. You can put anything inside. Apples. Berries. Chocolate.

Hearing about those crepes makes me think of baking, and how much I also like mixing flavors together in pies. For example, cranberries are too tart, but cranberries and apples are awesome together, as long as you use sweeter apples. My fingers itch to practice some mixing magic right now. But first, I write Mom and tell her about the Haunted House committee, how Keisha is learning a new trick, and how cute Maisie is, although she doesn't like hats. I don't say anything about how Hannah is the chair of the committee and is a very annoying boss, how I'm the only seventh-grade girl and I have to sit with a bunch of Sharpie Boys. There are some details that she just doesn't need to know.

I text Keisha. Usually, when she's at skating practice, she obviously can't be on her phone. But she always checks it during bathroom breaks.

Me: *It's set up!*

About forty-five minutes later, as I'm doing my math homework, she responds. *What's set up?*

Me: *You know what. The prank.*

Keisha: *Oh, that! You are crazy.*

Me: *Am not. How's practice today?*

Keisha: *Good. I need to stretch more. At least that's what Quinn said.*

Me: *Ewwww! I think he just wants to watch you stretch.*

Keisha: *Shut up!*

I send her hearts.

When Hannah gets back, she doesn't even acknowledge my existence, and I don't even look at her.

I'm not speaking to Hannah unless she speaks to me.

She stares at the money in her GeekGirlCon jar, then settles down on the bed and starts to draw in her sketchbook. Thankfully, she doesn't open up her backpack before or after dinner.

(I don't think she believes in homework.)

This means that she will definitely open her toilet-seat-stuffed binder during school tomorrow for maximum embarrassment.

Tomorrow can't come soon enough.

During dinner, I'm quiet while Dad and Kimberly talk about how excited they are about their real estate agent and how she already has great ideas of what houses to look at this weekend. I look down at my plate and carefully chew my food, centering myself to stay calm.

"You girls are welcome to tag along, although it might be best for you to wait until we whittle them down," says Dad.

"Michele, our agent, says to throw a wide net before eliminating," explains Kimberly.

I take another breath before saying, "Dad, I thought you had mentioned that maybe we could go apple picking this weekend."

Dad slaps his head. "Shoot. You're right. I didn't realize we'd be seeing houses all weekend. I thought it was just going to be Sunday. But Michele has us scheduled with appointments all day Saturday and Sunday." He gives me an apologetic look. "How about next weekend? Hopefully our realtor will give us a break."

"Well, I for one am going to be busy," says Hannah, and she launches into how she's the chair of the Haunted House committee. She talks about all of her ideas, including using lights from the drama department and also borrowing costumes from the community theater, where she has been in a lot of plays, including starring as Alice in *Alice in Wonderland*. I know because the first few times that I met her she told me all about it—and never once stopped to ask me about my interests or experiences.

"Aren't you also on the Haunted House committee?" asks Dad.

"Um, yeah," I say, cutting up my salad. It's kale, which is not my favorite. Mom usually gets Caesar salad kits, which are really yummy.

"So you get to work together!" says Kimberly.

"Yes," I say and give a smile that I'm sure wavers.

Hannah nods and pours herself water from the pitcher.

"It's great that you girls can work together, especially since you're in different grades," continues Kimberly. "You're getting a real chance to know each other outside the house."

"Absolutely," says Hannah, who suddenly beams at me. "I'm really looking forward to working with Lily."

What? This makes no sense.

But then I see her mother smiling at my dad. Oh, it's an act. After all, she is an actress.

Well, I can act, too!

"Ditto for me," I say. "I can't wait to spend more time working on the Haunted House with Hannah. It's going to be extra good this year."

Kimberly and Dad give each other another satisfied look. Like they've hit the jackpot.

I've never been a theater sort of person. But now, suddenly, I'm going to be a star of the stage. And the stage is going to be right in my own home.

The next morning, I'm walking down the hallway with Keisha like it's any other Thursday morning in my life, only it's not.

I have done something that's a complete first. I have pranked someone.

I'm not a pranking kind of person.

I'm seriously nice.

Buying Keisha polka-dot ribbons to go with her new skating outfit—that's a Lily thing.

Bringing in sunflowers for my flute teacher, Mrs. Chen, to contrast with her blue chair—that's a Lily thing.

Thinking about how toilet seat papers crinkle in the most embarrassing way doesn't seem like me.

"So any E spotting?" asks Keisha as we round the corner, past the band room.

"You remembered."

"I did." She drops her voice. "I used *the code*."

"The schedule gods don't have us cross paths too much."

"Well, he is an older man."

"Speaking of men, how is Quinn?"

"Please don't call him a man. It creeps me out."

"Okay, how is *the boy*?"

"He is fine, thank you. Fine looking. A fine skater. Just all of the above." She laughs. "I'm mostly angsting about what song to pick for my next routine. My coach has ideas. But her ideas"—she shrugs—"are a little overdone. She wants me to do 'Habanera' from *Carmen*, but really? It's nothing I have against that song. It's a classic. But I think every skater in the world has done it. Seriously. Every single one. And it's not going to be me." She shakes her head. "Uh-uh. Because I'm one of a kind."

"You are that," I admit.

"I have a month to figure it out. And it's stressing me out."

"A month? That seems like plenty of time."

"Not when it has to be the perfect song."

"I'm sure you'll find something perfect," I say. And

that's when, in the middle of the crowded hallway, Hannah grabs me by the arm.

"You!" she says. "I can't believe you'd do that! Really?"

"Do what?" I ask innocently. "You mean make your bed?" Kids weave around us in the packed hallway.

"No," says Hannah. "The toilet paper seat covers!"

Some sixth-grade boys swinging their trumpet cases slow down to stare at us.

"They sprang out at me during advisory," she hisses. "When I opened my binder to do my math homework."

"I thought you told your mom you didn't have math homework."

"Whatever." Hannah adjusts her backpack. Her face looks as red as a McIntosh apple. "I've got to go, but all I can say is, from now on, you really better watch out!"

She stalks off down the hall.

"Ew, she looks a little mad." Keisha stops to talk a drink of water at the fountain. "You've really started something now, Lily."

The next day, on Friday, in social studies, I pull out my binder and gawk. Someone has written, *I love Ethan!* straight across it.

I try to wipe it off with a tissue, only it's not working. "No way!" I moan.

"What's wrong?" asks Reese, who sits behind me. Unfortunately, I can't seem to shake him.

"Nothing," I say, throwing my body like a human shield over the binder. Only I do it so fast that my binder drops onto the floor with a loud *whomp*.

I swear half the kids whip around to stare at me.

I go to scoop up my binder, but Reese beats me to it. "No!" I blurt.

"Magic, why are you freaking out?" asks Reese, handing me the binder.

Don't look. Don't look. Don't look.

Shaking his head, he grins at me until he peers down at my binder. "Oh," he says.

He tosses the binder back onto my desk like it's a Frisbee.

"Stop playing around back there," says my teacher, Mrs. Rinalducci. "If you two want to flirt, please do it on your own time."

"I'm not flirting," I say, my face reddening. I can tell that not one kid in the class believes me. After all, most girls think that Reese is one of the cutest boys in the seventh grade.

"Is something wrong then?" asks Mrs. Rinalducci,

"Someone wrote on my binder," I say, because I don't want Reese to think I wrote that. Not that I care what Reese thinks.

"Someone from our class?" Her eyes lift to Reese's.

"No," I say in small voice.

Mrs. Rinalducci holds up a small bottle. "I have a cleaner just for these kind of emergencies." My face warms at the thought of my teacher reading *I love Ethan!*

"That's okay," I say. "I think it's permanent. I'll just borrow some loose-leaf paper,"

"You can have some of mine," offers Reese. And I'm not sure why he's being so weirdly nice.

After school, the Haunted House committee meets. I'm a little nervous since I'm worried that word has somehow gotten back to Ethan about the binder incident. And the truth is—I'm mad.

My prank was just silly—I didn't give away some kind of personal information! What Hannah did was different. Maybe I should say something to her?

But Hannah's not at the meeting, which is strange since she's supposed to be leading it.

A few minutes later, I find myself sitting with Reese and his friends again.

Sure, there's a seat next to Ethan, but there's no way I'm going to have a repeat of last Wednesday. But I do get daring and, from across the way, I give Ethan a wave.

He waves back! And says, "Hi, Lily."

Ethan said hi.

He remembered my name.

Suddenly, the day doesn't seem so bad after all. Everyone chats as we wait for Hannah to show up.

"I guess we better get started without our fearless leader," says Lindsay.

"And I guess that means voting on what we're doing," says Thanh Ha.

"Vote! Vote! Vote!" chants Reese as he bangs on the table. He's joined by his friends and the sixth graders.

"Okay," Thanh Ha waves her hand for quiet. "Uh, we sort of have a problem. I have no idea what we're voting on. Did anyone take notes? Please say yes. Please say yes!"

I raise my hand and feel a sense of pride swell in my chest. "I did." I always take notes.

"Way to go, Magic!" shouts Reese and he gives me a thumbs-up.

"Magic?" Behind his glasses, Ethan's eyebrows rise in confusion.

"It's Lily's real name," jokes Reese. "Her nickname is Lily."

"Really?" Ethan's eyebrows now meet in a unibrow.

"It's a joke." I can't believe that I'm explaining this. "Although not one that anyone understands."

"Someday," says Reese with a little grin. Oh, he drives me crazy!

I read off all of the ideas. And then, heads down on the tables, we all raise our hands to vote for the different scenes. I vote for a zoo for people, a graveyard scene, the crazy butcher, and zombie high.

I pray that the bad smells room, aka the fart zone, doesn't win. "Okay, time to announce the winners. Everyone be quiet," says Lindsay.

"She better say mad scientist lab," says Jonah, "or else I'm really going to be mad."

"Okay, do you people not understand the word *quiet*?" says Thanh Ha.

"Definitely not," says Reese.

"The winners are . . ." says Lindsay, pausing dramatically. "A graveyard scene, the zombie high, a mad scientist lab, and witch's lair."

Everyone whose scene got picked looks really happy.

Jonah claps, clearly excited. "I really, *really* want to do the mad scientist lab."

"You could combine the mad scientist lab with the crazy butcher because you could have a mad scientist decapitate someone," says Ethan, looking up from his phone.

"That's awesome," says Jonah. Of course it is.

Ethan pushes up his glasses. He doesn't even need to pay attention because he's coming up with great ideas.

Suddenly Hannah barrels into the library. "Sorry I'm late," she huffs. "I couldn't get my locker open. It got jammed and I had to find a custodian, which was impossible. And then I forgot what side of the library we were meeting on."

How did she forget? The library isn't that big.

"So." Hannah whips out the pieces of paper with our ideas. "I'm ready to start the vote."

"We already voted," I say, because I can't help myself.

"What?" Hannah's voice screeches. Putting her hand on her chest, she takes a breath. "Sorry, you guys. I was just running. So I'm a little out of breath." Suddenly she smiles sweetly, especially at Lindsay, Thanh Ha, and Ethan. "Did Lily have you guys vote?" She says it pleasantly, but underneath I can hear the daggers in her voice.

"Nope!" says a sixth grader.

"I did," says Lindsay. "Since I figured we needed to get started."

"Oh." Hannah's forehead relaxes. "Awesome idea, Lindsay! Thanks so much."

Thanh Ha holds up the sheet with the winning ideas.

"So no movie themes?" says Hannah, who's clearly upset. "I thought we had discussed doing horror movie scenes."

"I think *you* had discussed it," I say. "But I don't think it was actually an idea we were voting on."

"Sorry about that," says Lindsay. "Should we vote again?"

I know that Hannah wants to, but surprisingly she shakes her head. "No, it's fine. Those are great ideas. Next we need to decide who is going to be in what scene and what will happen. Last year at the community theater, I was Alice in *Alice in Wonderland*, so I know a few things about creating stagecraft."

She just had to get that in.

"So," continues Hannah, "in order to make all of this happen, we're going to work in partners. I volunteer to play a vampire host escorting our guests around. At the community theater, they have awesome vampire costumes. And happily"—she claps her hands—"there's one that would fit Ethan perfectly. So he'll be my partner."

Of course he will.

"Lindsay and I want to be zombies," says Thanh Ha, holding Lindsay's hand. Those two do everything together.

"Yes!" says Hannah like she's the president of the universe.

Jonah's arm shoot up. "I'm going to be the guy in the mad scientist lab who gets his head chopped off."

"A member of the Talking Heads," says Reese, cracking himself up.

"Huh?" says Ethan. "I don't get it."

"It's an old band that my dad really likes," says Reese. "The Talking Heads, so it's a joke."

"Okay, cool," says Ethan. His pushes his bright, shiny blond hair off his forehead in such a cute way. . . .

One of the sixth graders, a tall one with the mole says, "We want to be ghosts in the graveyard scene."

"Awesome! So that leaves just the witch scene," says Hannah. She looks directly at me. "You can be the witch, Lily."

"And what about me?" asks Reese.

"You can be . . ."

"A frog?" suggests Reese. "Get it, Magic? Or maybe a rat." Then he snaps his fingers. "Hey, I got it. It'd be perfect. I want to be a demented clown. It's much more me."

"Go for it," says Hannah.

A witch. I'm playing a witch. In a scene with Reese, a clown. How perfect.

Now the question is, who is the real witch?

It's an easy answer.

Chapter Ten
TART AND NOT SWEET

Saturday morning, I've propped my planner on my knees when there's a knock on the door. At noon, in my schedule, I have circled *Chat with Mom*. Before that, at 9:00, work on my social studies essay, then math, then at 11:00 a.m.: *Check out more pie videos*.

"Shiny and no whiny!" calls out Kimberly.

I have no idea what this means.

Hannah pushes herself to a sitting position in her bed and rubs her eyes.

"Hannah, shiny and no whiny!" calls Kimberly once again.

"I'm shining!" says Hannah. I guess it means time

to get up? Or be happy? Hannah's eyes are still half-shut so I'm not going to try and find out.

The door creaks open, and Kimberly has on her biker pants and shirt. She and my dad have already been out on their morning ride. She smiles at me. "Lily, your dad's wiping the water off the wheel rims of our bikes. It started to rain pretty consistently." Her eyes land on my planner. "Looks like you're busy."

I shrug. "Just trying to stay ahead."

"Hannah, are you taking notes?" asks Kimberly.

"Ha ha." From across the room, Hannah groans as she opens up her dresser and ferrets out sweats.

Kimberly glances down at her watch. "Hannah, hurry up. You know Coach Coz makes you do extra laps if you're late."

"Okay, okay."

"You realize that you can move into the Platinum group. That the Junior Olympics are a shoo-in."

"I know, Mom."

After quite a bit of drawer slamming, Hannah drags herself out of the room, with her swim team bag slung over her shoulder. She shockingly says bye to me. Probably because Kimberly is watching.

A couple of hours later, after doing my homework

and pie research, I video chat with Mom. I've been waiting for this all week. We're going to bake an apple pie together. Well, I'm going to bake and she's going to give advice.

With her on the screen on the family laptop in the kitchen, it will almost be like we're in the same room. The connection is clear and Mom looks relaxed and happy. Today, she's wearing this beautiful teal shawl around her shoulders.

"I bought it at the souk. That's an outdoor market-place," she says, patting the shawl. "It was made on a hand loom. It's so soft and silky. I wish you could touch it."

"I know." That would be mean I'd actually be with my mom in person.

Mom glances at the quarter cup of brown sugar, the teaspoon of cinnamon, quarter of a teaspoon of salt, and ground nutmeg that I already premeasured. "I think you don't have enough brown sugar. I like to have a little more on hand, in case the apples are a bit too tart."

"Are you sure?"

"No, I'm not. You'll have to taste test the apples." Not a problem! I cut up a Granny Smith and Honeycrisp and taste them. "Oh my gosh, Mom, you're so right.

The Granny Smiths are extra tart." I blink at her. "How did you know?"

"I could smell them," she jokes.

I add a bit more brown sugar.

She asks me what I've up to as I peel apples. "I'm definitely not nearly as fast as you," I say.

"That's fine. The judges won't know if you've peeled something fast or not."

"True."

"So what's up?"

I tell her about how Keisha is going crazy trying to find the perfect song for her new routine. And how flute is going well. "So far so good, although I might be ready for an intermediation flute."

"Congratulations," says Mom. It's taking me forever to peel and slice the apples. "How do you slice faster?" I asked.

"It comes with practice. Better to work on accuracy than speed." Mom stares at her hands.

"About the new flute," says Mom. "Do you need it right away?"

"Eventually but not immediately. By next year."

"Good because I'm not making very much here. Just a stipend. And Dad's business is just starting."

"I get it. I can wait."

"If that's really frustrating to you let me know. I could probably ask Grandma for money."

"It's okay." I throw the apple slices into the colander. This is so that the apples release their juices and the pie won't be too runny.

"That pie is going to be good. I can just tell!"

"Me too." I'm hoping. And for a moment, I'm quietly trying to let hope puff inside of me like very flaky piecrust.

"Are you adjusting okay"—Mom pauses—"to everyone living together?"

"It's fine." I take a deep breath and consider actually telling her about Hannah. Maybe I could launch into it by first telling her the good news. "I'm fully moved into my room with Hannah, and my bed is comfortable."

"That's great, Lily," says Mom. "At first, I thought you were going to tell me something horrible, like you were sleeping in the basement or something."

"No, nothing like that—"

"I'd feel horrible if you girls weren't getting along. You're so mature and thoughtful. I knew there was no need for me to worry." She blows kisses at me.

"Yeah, there's really no need for you to worry." Inwardly, I sigh.

There's no way I can tell her now. Even about the little things. Like the way that Hannah and Kimberly seem to have secret words. How Hannah's stuff is creeping all over my desk. In fact, I can't even sit at my desk. And how she laughed when she saw that someone wrote *hi* on my backpack in orange (which was probably one of the Sharpies Boys). How Hannah borrowed my shirt without asking. Her general awfulness on the Haunted House committee. It all makes me so mad!

"I can tell something's wrong, Lily," says Mom like she can read my mind. "You can tell me."

Not really.

Instead I tell her about some of my frustrations with Dad. I figure it's familiar territory. "I've been trying to get Dad to go apple picking," I say. "I really want to use fresh apples to bake with, especially for the Fall Festival contest. But he's always busy with Kimberly looking at open houses. It's so annoying. Even right now as we speak, they're already out with their real estate agent."

"You know, it's wonderful your dad's at a differ-ent place now. That his video business is going well, finally. I'm thrilled he's ready to buy a house." Wow! I expected Mom to say that's typical Dad, always unavailable. She adds, "I wish I could be there to take you apple picking."

"Me too," I admit.

chapter eleven
A LOT TO SNEEZE AT

I can't believe we've been in school for two weeks now. It's been super busy with lots of homework and new music in band. For the past week, things have been really crazy. For example, a few days ago, Hannah ate all the grapes I had just washed and set down in a bowl to snack on. I somehow seem to be missing some of my clothes, especially socks, and it's Hannah's chore to do the laundry. Then this morning the contents of my backpack were spilled all over my floor.

It has to have been Hannah!

I curl my toes. I clench my jaw and bite my lip, literally.

I decide to talk to Dad about my stepsister problem. It's a Sunday afternoon, and he's in his office, perusing footage he just shot of a scrimmage football game. Navigating my way around some tripods, I clear my throat.

"Dad, do you have a minute?"

He glances up from the screen. "Sure thing. I've got a few before a client call. What's up?"

I pause. This isn't easy. "I wanted to talk to you about Hannah."

"Oh, the bedroom. I know. She's not exactly neat." He glances at file folders on the floor. And his cluttered bookshelf filled with videography guides and spy novels. "I'm certainly not one to talk. Hopefully, you'll be a good influence on both of us. I know that poor Kimberly does her best."

I try again. "Hannah doesn't seem"—I pause—"exactly happy."

"I know. She's not like you, my happy girl. Kimberly says she's always had difficulty with transitions. It'll all work out. Sharing the room. School."

I want to say that it isn't working and it won't work out, but Dad's cell buzzes. And I'm feeling guilty because I'm supposed to be his happy girl. He blows me a kiss and says he'll talk to me later.

After school on Monday, all the committees meet in the library. Our committee is supposed to decide what will happen in each of our scenes. The Fall Festival is now three and a half weeks away.

Hannah's surrounded by kids asking her questions about what we're doing today. That's because there's no agenda or schedule. Then she taps her chair. "Lily, come sit down with us."

What? She's asking me to sit with the eighth graders? Not just sit but in the seat next to Ethan? We must have crossed into some alternate upside-down world.

"Okay, Lily," she whispers. "Can you tell me what I said we were going to do? I know you wrote it all down in that planner."

Right now it's hard for me to concentrate. I'm so hyperaware of Ethan—he's pulling his phone out of his pocket.

"Sure, Hannah," I say in an equally sweet voice. "I'm so happy to help my big sister out."

"Step," corrects Hannah.

"Only there's no step between us," I say. "We're"—I cross my fingers behind my back—"so close." Ethan nods, looking impressed.

"It's true," says Hannah. "We even share a room."

As soon as Ethan goes back to looking at his phone, Hannah lowers her voice. "Show me the notebook," she hisses.

"Sure, Hannah, *big sis*," I say in a loud enthusiastic voice. "I'm happy to show you my notebook so you can see what you said we're doing this week. Since you forgot and I wrote it all down." I smile.

Hannah's smile grows taut. "That's great since I asked you to take notes, *little sis*." Oh, wow. She's a better liar than I am.

"Actually, I must have not heard you. I must have been"—I tap my head—"reading your mind." I whip out my planner. "Today, we're still brainstorming our scenes with our partners."

"Yes, of course. I knew that. I just wanted to see my exact words. Actually, today we're going to write out our scenes so"—she waves her own blank notebook—"everyone know exactly what we're doing."

"Actually, you said we were just going to brainstorm our scenes with our partners. But that we could swap partners." She can have Reese and I'll take Ethan, thank you very much! I peer down at my notes. "I wrote it down word for word."

"There's note swapping," she says. "And brainstorming, yes. But writing and brainstorming. It's the same thing."

"Not really," says Ethan. "When you brainstorm, you often throw away the lame answers."

"Exactly," I say. Oh, wow, Ethan and I are thinking alike!

That's when Hannah stands up and claps her hands. "Okay, everyone. I want you to figure out exactly what will happen with your partner." She points over at Ethan. "So I'm going to be the vampire princess." She flicks back her hair. "And I'll have these really long fake black nails with jewels and a velvet cape—really, actually, since we have those clothes in the costume shop. Anyway, I'll point and say to Ethan, 'I vant you to suck your blood.' And he'll flap his wings and lean over with his fangs, dripping with blood like he's going to bite someone's neck."

She spins and flips her hair again. "Plus, I'll put in a little vampire twirl."

"Isn't the point to scare people?" I say.

"Yes, but it's also to entertain people. You do want to be original. Or would you prefer to be boring? Plus, we're the tour guides."

She gazes over at Ethan who's looking at his phone. "What do you think?"

"Huh?"

"About what I just said."

"It's good," he says. I can totally tell he wasn't listening to her. This makes me feel happy. But then I realize he wasn't exactly listening to me, either.

"Maybe we should just yawn." Reese points to his mouth. "When I open my mouth really wide, you can see my tonsils. That's scary." I can't help but giggle.

"Maybe we do something between scaring and entertaining," suggests Thanh Ha.

"With an emphasis on scaring," says a sixth grader.

We sit down and try to come up with scenarios.

Reese wants us to have a really scary witch's kitchen. We argue a bit about whether it should be a classic witch's den or something else. Reese wants it to be an ultra-modern kitchen.

"You know, scary, but futuristic," he explains.

We finally settle on something in between: a classic witch's kitchen but with some creepy electronic sounds in addition to lightning. And then we actually, amazingly, have fun planning it out.

Everyone goes around and gives a brief overview of what their scene will look like. Then we have to write out a prop and costume list so we'll know what we all need.

"I'm going to assign everyone jobs," says Hannah. "I'm going to be in charge of buying snacks. And making the signs. Ethan will be in charge of buying drinks. And also filming."

Then she goes through all of these cool jobs like someone ordering pizza. That's Lindsay's job. The sixth-grader group get to buy scary props. And Reese gets to buy gummy worms, spaghetti, and other gross stuff for the witch's brew. Luke gets to buy prizes to give to the little kids, and Jonah is in charge of safe but scary-looking props to saw off his head.

"Lily's job is prop inventory," announces Hannah.

"What's that?" I ask.

"There's two giant boxes of old props someone found from ten years ago. You get to through it all and figure out what we have." She smiles sweetly. "I hope you don't have allergies. Because they're super dusty."

I look over at Ethan, who is on his phone. I bet he's watching videos to give him ideas. "Even if I had allergies, which I don't, I'll be fine."

Then I smile like I love inventory. Like taking inventory of dusty boxes all by myself is exactly what I wanted to do with the rest of my life. "I can make an inventory list using Excel or something."

"Isn't that a little much?" says Reese.

"No," I say with a huff.

"Reese, shut up," says Hannah, which makes no sense. There's no way she's coming to my rescue. Not when she tried to give me the worst job.

"Next week we'll be meeting at Ethan's," she continues, "and everyone should bring snacks so it'll be a party."

What? We. Are. Meeting. *At Ethan's?*

I immediately text Keisha to tell her the amazing news. And the bad news. While organizing is up my alley, I know Hannah gave me a bunch of super dusty boxes as a punishment. But suddenly I figure out how to punish her with the perfect prank.

Chapter Twelve
JUST DESSERTS

For a solid week, I do normal things like brush my teeth, talk to Keisha about songs for her routine, do my homework, work on baking, play with Maisie, and try to teach her to sit using a hand command. And for a solid week, Hannah sneers at me and does everything possible to make me feel unwelcome in my own room.

It doesn't work.

Well, maybe it works for a few seconds. But the entire time I'm thinking all of these wonderful things that will cancel out her meanness and snarkiness. That's because *I, Lily Reta Silvers, get to go to Ethan Sanarov's house.* And while I'm there not only do I get to see Ethan in his natural habitat . . .

(As in the place where he actually lives.)

But I will also get to perform a prank on Hannah that will restore justice to the world.

Sometimes I have to trick myself into not thinking about it so I can do my homework and go to sleep and breathe. So I'm really grateful for chores.

I'm even happy to dig into the big, super dusty inventory box so that I keep my mind busy. Counting prizes that makes me sneeze keeps me from thinking this one thought.

I'm going to Ethan's house. I'm going to Ethan's house. And Hannah will get her just desserts.

I figure out how to use the Excel program on my dad's computer and put everything into a spreadsheet. I'm actually proud of myself. Sure, I'm sneezing a lot but that's what tissues are for.

Excel is seriously awesome. It isn't just that it looks neat with all of these columns, but it actually does math for you.

Finally, after what seems like an eternity—but is actually only seven days—it's the night before I'll be going to Ethan's. I must prepare.

Not by taking a shower or planning my outfit or doing my hair—I much prefer to take showers in the morning because the pillow and my hair don't always get along. Whatever great style my hair had at night completely disappears by the morning. So morning showers only for me.

Instead, the night is all about my prank: Oreos and toothpaste. It's a classic for a reason. And I figured out a way so that only Hannah will eat the Crest-filled Oreo. I race into the bathroom and find white toothpaste. Back in the kitchen, I grab an Oreo, scrape out the cream, then start to replace it with toothpaste. All I need is one Oreo for my prank.

That's when Dad pads into the kitchen. "Hey, Lily, how about we go apple picking this weekend?"

"Sounds great, Dad." He eyes the toothpaste. He eyes the cookies. Uh-oh!

I grab the toothpaste and hold it up. "Couldn't find the toothpaste anywhere. Now I know where it was."

"I heard you and wanted to check-in." He pauses. "To see how things are going? School. Living here."

Now he wants to talk?

"I'm spending a lot of time with Hannah and getting to know her really well," I say, which isn't a lie. "So things are heading in a good direction." Because this prank is going to be really amazing.

"Happy to hear it. Anything else?"

"Nope." Other than things are about to get fresh between me and Hannah? Minty fresh! "Night, Dad."

"Goodnight, Lily."

The plastic crinkles as I finish putting the cookies back into the package.

It's going to be a very good day.

The day of Ethan's planning party (because that's really what it is!), I stare at the alarm clock in disbelief. It's 7:30 a.m. I have way overslept and only have fifteen minutes to get ready and eat breakfast. A shower is not possible.

How could this happen? I know I set my alarm!

I wanted to look perfect since we are going to be meeting at Ethan's right after school.

Rushing into the kitchen, I see Hannah, Dad, and Kimberly eating at the table. Unlike me, they're fully dressed. Dad and Kimberly both wear biking pants and shirts, both ready for their morning rides.

"Did someone mess with my alarm clock?" I glare at Hannah, who's in a hoodie, jeans, and what looks like my socks.

"I wouldn't even know how," says Hannah, who

spoons in her last bite of granola. That is clearly such a lie; she's a whiz on her iPad.

"Why didn't anyone wake me?!" I want to kick over the trash. Hannah looks so relaxed right now.

"Lily, I just assumed you were fussing with yourself in the mirror," says Kimberly. "You're always the first one up, so I didn't check."

"Ditto." Hannah walks her bowl to the sink.

"Lily, it's not like you to oversleep," says Dad.

"I know. It's not like me." It's like someone else. Hannah! I want to scream her name so badly, but I hold my tongue. Right now it's my word against hers.

"Well, you better hurry up and get dressed," says Kimberly. "If you want to make the bus."

I race to pick out an outfit for school, but there's almost no clothing in my dresser. Last night Hannah was supposed to do the laundry. I check and see that all of my clothes are still sitting in the washer, damp and probably mildewy. They've been in the washer for hours. *Arghhhhh!*

Not today!

I end up wearing dirty clothes from my hamper.

Hannah has to know how important this day is. I

actually get to go *inside of Ethan's home*. I've passed by it before. I know the address by heart: 2413 Oak Tree Lane.

When we're alone in the hallway before we leave for the bus, I say to Hannah, "I know you turned off my alarm!"

"I don't know what you're talking about," she says all innocently.

"You do, too!"

"Lily, please," says Dad from the kitchen. "There's no reason to yell."

Oh yes there is! Hannah has provoked me on purpose, so that my dad and Kimberly will overhear and think I'm the one causing the problem, not her. That I'm too demanding, just like my mom—or how Dad thought she was when they were married.

"We're not going to stand for fighting," says Dad, appearing in the hallway. "If you girls can't work it out, we'll have to work it out for you. No more fighting, or we're taking away your phones."

Kimberly peers around Dad, a mug of coffee in her hands. "If that doesn't work, you'll be grounded."

"It's not my fault. Lily is freaking out," says Hannah sweetly.

"Actually, it is," I say.

"Girls," Dad warns. "What did I just say?"

I'm so mad I don't dare say another word because my eruption would be epic. And I can't. I just can't.

Instead, I walk away.

Later, when I get to school, Keisha says to me in advisory, "Are you okay?"

Before I can say anything, Reese calls out. "Hey, Magic, didn't you wear that skirt yesterday? And shirt, too?"

My face warms. But then it comes to me. I know exactly what I should do. Swooping around, I smile and calmly say, "Looks like you notice what I wear, Reese. *And* you have a special nickname for me. What's that about?"

Now it's his turn to blush.

I feel like high-fiving myself, only I don't have to because Jonah comes up to me and gives me a high five.

"Good one," he says.

"Aren't you supposed to be his friend?"

"Exactly," says Jonah. "That's why it's a good one."

"Can you please tell me why he calls me Magic."

Solemnly, Jonah holds up his hand. "I took a vow. I can never tell you why."

"A vow? Are you serious?"

He glances over at Reese. "Very."

"You guys are so weird."

"Thanks," says Jonah.

While Mr. Pastcan takes role, Keisha asks me if I want to travel with her family to an ice-skating competition in Portland. "It's going to be so fun. There's a really amazing hotel that we've booked. It would be a road trip! And they have an indoor pool with a waterslide."

"That sounds awesome. I really, really want to go. But my dad's taking me apple picking all day on Saturday. We've been talking about it forever and it's finally happening."

Keisha bites her lip.

"You're not mad?" I say.

"No, having you would have just been a bonus. But I'm glad that you'll be able to spend time with your dad."

"Yeah, I think maybe it would be a good time to tell him a little bit about what's really happening between me and Hannah." I tell Keisha about the alarm clock.

I'm going to get Hannah so good. I whisper what I'm planning to do with the Oreos in her ear.

Keisha yelps. "No! Don't do it!" She vigorously shakes her head. "Lily, please. Something terrible will happen to you. Look at me. Just *look* at me. You need to stop this fight."

"Well, I didn't start it. She did. And I'm not standing by and letting something happen to me. I'm doing something about it, in a *big* way."

Keisha throws up her hands. "Then you'll be stupid in a big way."

"Do I say you're being stupid when you try tricks on the skating rink that are super hard?"

"No." She sighs.

"Then you need to trust I can do it."

"It's not that I don't trust you," says Keisha. "You're my best friend."

"Don't you always say that when you skate you need to believe in yourself? To trust that your feet know what to do it and not to overthink?"

"That's different. It's a competition."

"What's happening between me and Hannah is no different," I say. "It's exactly that—a competition."

After school, all I can think about is Keisha's words to me. Was I being stupid? Should I just end this right now?

Maybe I should.

Maybe Keisha was right.

I can barely remember the walk to Ethan's house, since I'm thinking so hard. In my backpack I have everything I need for the prank to work.

I have to remain confident but I'm feeling nervous.

Just like Keisha always wins her skating competitions, I am going to win mine. She isn't going to be the only successful competitor around here.

The Haunted House committee walks the three blocks from school to Ethan's house, a craftsman bungalow, and the front yard is tidy with nice foliage. I bet there will be wood-paneled walls inside with rows of built-in bookshelves. Maybe antique furniture, a woodstove, and a Persian carpet.

When we go inside, the house is ultramodern and much bigger-looking than I had expected. Walls have been knocked down for a large spacious kitchen and great room. There's a full-screen TV where a long time ago a fireplace might have been.

Ethan's mom greets us and says to put any snacks right on the coffee table. She looks just like Ethan with those amazing green eyes. I try not to stare at her and act casual, like this is just a normal day.

On the coffee table, I consider wedging my package of Oreos between a bowl of M&M's and a bowl of tortilla chips but think better of it. The first cookie in the package is the one I replaced with mint toothpaste. What if someone else takes it?

Instead, I secure the cookies safely on my lap.

Soon enough, all of the committee members are sitting around on the couches or comfortable chairs. Ethan plops down onto a love seat. For a moment, I consider sitting down next to him, but Hannah waltzes in front of me and promptly squeezes in beside him.

"Hi, everyone," I say, managing to make direct eye contact with Ethan and avoiding Hannah. He's wearing a blue-striped long-sleeve t-shirt that contrasts nicely with his shiny blond hair. As always, Ethan looks really good.

As I sit down in a chair across from Lindsay, it hits me: Maybe Hannah isn't acting all flirty with Ethan to get at me. What if she likes him? Or what if it's both?

Right now, she's laughing at something that Ethan is saying. Laughing way too hard because Ethan isn't really that funny, not like Reese. I turn to Lindsay, who's knitting in the chair next to me. Her needles rhythmically clack together.

"Is that something for the Haunted House?" I ask.

She laughs. "Nope. It's a scarf. I just need something to do with my hands."

Suddenly, I feel something *ping* against the back of my neck. Then something else hits my lap. I peer down. It's a blue M&M.

"Go ahead, Magic. Eat it," says Reese. He sits on the floor right next to the M&M's. Why hadn't I noticed him before?

Because of Ethan. When Ethan's in the room, it's like everyone else gets blurry and out of focus.

"It's melting, better eat it, Magic."

"Ha ha, Reese!" I sputter. And for some reason my face warms.

I bite my lip.

Everyone digs into the snacks now. The sixth graders have already scooped out half of the peanuts.

"Time to open up the Oreos," I announce.

Reese catapults toward me and starts to stuff his hand into the package of Oreos.

"No!" I yell. "The head of the committee gets served first, of course."

I step over to Hannah. "Oreo?" I ask, keeping my voice even.

"Sure!" she says.

With great satisfaction, I hand Hannah the toothpaste-filled Oreo, and she places it on a napkin.

Yes. It will just be a matter of time.

Seconds even.

In a happy daze, I set the package of regular, non-minty Oreos down onto the coffee table. "Help yourself, everyone!" I announce.

Reese immediately pounces on them and takes, like, five.

"Wow. Just a little hungry?" I laugh.

"Oh yeah," says Reese. "I'm a growing boy."

"Okay, quiet, everyone," says Hannah, which feels more like she's personally shushing me, but I don't care. Because right at this moment, her hand is brushing delightfully close to her minty cookie. "We really need to start the meeting." She gives her fake, I'm-a-nice-person smile. "Today, we're going to give an update on our jobs. Nothing like dividing and conquering."

"I thought you said we were going to discuss our scripts," says Samir. He nods over at his other sixth-grader friends. "'Cause we got some scary plans."

"We'll do that next week," explains Hannah.

I can tell she totally forgot about going over the scripts.

She picks up her Oreo. Then she looks at Ethan. "Want mine? I ate before I came." Oh. No! No!

Ethan shakes his head. "Nah, I'm all good."

I mentally let out a huge sigh of relief.

"So let's everyone give an update on your jobs." As Hannah calls out people's names, I'm starting to have second thoughts.

What am doing? What if she swallows all of that toothpaste at once? What if her mouth starts foaming? What if she throws up Crest all over Ethan's mom's brand-new-looking couch?

I should tell her that the cookie fell on the floor and not to eat it.

I start to sweat a little as Samir announces that the sixth graders successfully scrounged up huge boxes to use as gravestones.

Reese and his friends mention how they went through their Halloween costumes to find plastic axes and stuff. Lindsay and Thanh Ha said they made a trip to the fabric store together to get find cloth to use as a backdrop.

"Ethan and I went to the community theater together," announces Hannah with a smug grin. "You know, to borrow some props from the costume room."

They did?

Then she looks at me. "Lily, how were those dusty boxes of props?"

"Good, actually," I say, and I whip out my spreadsheet. "I put the inventory list into Excel."

Some of the kids look at me like I'm totally crazy.

"Uh, sounds like you went a little overboard?" says Hannah.

"No, made it much easier, actually."

"Okay, whatever."

Why isn't Hannah eating the cookie?

She goes over timelines. How we should do our tasks by next week blah blah and blah and I'm giving up hope.

When suddenly Hannah bites into her Oreo and groans. She winces like she just sucked a lemon dry.

"What's wrong?" asks Thanh Ha.

"Someone can't handle her Oreos," jokes Reese.

Hannah fans her mouth as if it's on fire.

I didn't put hot peppers in there. Sheesh. Hannah grabs a napkin, turns her head to spit out the cookie.

Thanh Ha quickly glances at Ethan. "Where's your bathroom?" she asks.

Ethan points toward the hall. "First door to the left."

Hannah darts to the bathroom. I can hear the faucet running.

"There's a stomach flu going around," says Samir.

Oh, it's definitely not the stomach flu.

Hannah lumbers back into the living room and gives me dagger eyes.

"Are you okay?" I ask innocently.

"Fine," says Hannah. "I ate a really weird Oreo."

"Maybe it's a ghoul scout cookie," suggests Reese.

"And poisoned," adds Jonah.

"Yeah, by a witch," says Hannah and her eyes cut into me.

"I'm not touching those Oreos," says Thanh Ha.

Reese grabs another handful. "More for me then." He bites into his. "Mmmm. Creamy vanilla."

"Personally, I love mint," I say.

"That's good to know," says Hannah. "Very good."

And in that moment, I realize that I've gone too far, and that I'm going to get it.

Sooner or later.

Probably sooner.

Chapter Thirteen
MONSTROUS REVENGE

A couple of days later, nothing has happened to me. No bucket of wet paint tipping onto my head. No chocolate pudding in my shoes. No heart-shaped helium balloons that say *Lily Loves Ethan* delivered to school.

I'm starting to think that maybe Hannah has forgotten about her threat.

It's school picture day, and so far I've changed my outfit about three times. At first, I tried a t-shirt with flared sleeves and a pair of jeans, then a teal dress, then a skirt, and now I'm back to jeans. Before breakfast, I read Mom's latest text. She tells me she's learning to be very careful about complimenting people in Morocco.

You'll never believe what happened. I complimented this woman's scarf yesterday. Immediately, she pulled it right off her neck and gave it to me! She insisted I keep it!

I think about what would happen at school if each time Keisha and I complimented each other, we had to give up that item. We'd be swapping clothes back and forth all of the time.

When I brush my teeth after breakfast, I notice the toothpaste is greener than usual after I spit it out.

"What's this?" Inspecting my teeth, I see they're green!

I spit again, and no matter how many times I rinse, my teeth stay green! Not just my teeth—my lips and tongue, too!

"Something happened to the toothpaste!" I shriek.

Hannah pokes her head into the bathroom. "Oh, really? Imagine that. Toothpaste messing up something." She drums on her chin. "Hmmm. Like Oreos."

"This is different!"

I start to say something more when Kimberly walks in.

"Girls, is there something wrong?" she asks.

Yes! I want to scream.

But I stop myself and press my lips together so she won't notice the color.

If I tell on Hannah about this, she'll tell on me about my Oreo escapade. With both of our warnings already, I don't want to even think about what would happen.

Probably no phone for a week.

Or being grounded, which would mean no going to the Haunted House committee and no seeing Ethan.

I shake my head, lips held as tight as possible.

When I arrive at school, I see Reese and his friends huddled outside like penguins trying to shield themselves from the wind. Only it's late September and we live in Washington and the wind is just a breeze, even if there is a slight chill to the air.

"Hey, it's Magic!" shouts Jonah, nudging Reese.

When another one of Reese's buddies shout out, "Magic!" I ignore him. Anyway, the last thing I need is for Reese or one of his pals to comment on my green mouth and lips.

At school, as much as I wipe my mouth, my lips still look very greenish. I pretty much stay quiet all day, pointing to my neck like I have a sore throat if anyone asks me a question.

For my school picture, I borrow some of Keisha's colored lip gloss, and I don't show my teeth. Despite the color of my tongue, which no one has seen yet, I think I'm looking almost okay.

Right after the photo is taken, on my way to third period, I see Ethan. Through the crowded halls, he steps closer to me. Behind him, on the bulletin board, I see the poster that Hannah designed for the Fall Festival.

Raising his eyebrows, Ethan says, "Hey, Lily."

Wow. This is the first time he's acknowledged me in the hallway. His voice is so deep, he sounds like he could be in high school.

I want to say, "Hi, Ethan." Instead, I nod. There's nooooooo way I'm opening my mouth.

He smiles at me really warmly. Then Ethan slows down like he wants to talk to me!

Arghhhhh! Really? Today?! Reluctantly, I speed up like I have to be someplace really important.

Hannah is really going to get it now.

Later, during lunch, when I tell Keisha about what happened with my missed opportunity with Ethan, she agrees it was a complete tragedy.

By the afternoon, my green teeth and lips have

disappeared, but that doesn't stop me from initiating Operation Get-Hannah-Back. I download an app, the one that I once overheard Reese and his friends talking about. It's a notification prank app. Basically, you pick a victim, and the person receives a phone notification from an official-sounding source saying something like it's a snow day. There are also silly options, like telling a person they have bad breath, but those don't fit what I'm thinking.

I send Hannah the one that says it's school Pajama Day.

The next morning, when Hannah wakes up, I'm in my striped flannel pajamas.

"Aren't you getting dressed?" she asks. It's 7:10. By 6:45, I'm almost always in the shower.

"Already showered." I lean down to pet Maisie, who's lying at the foot of my bed. I tap my plaid flannel pajama top. "This is what I'm wearing to school. It's Pajama Day."

"Are you sure?" her voice sounds doubtful.

"One hundred percent. It's a pre-Spirit Week thing." I shrug.

Hannah checks her phone. "Hey, you're right! I got a notification!" When she puts on her Cookie Monster pajamas, I try not to crack up.

Dad and Kimberly say we look really cute, and Kimberly says we should take stuffed animals.

Hannah decides to take her giant frog, Mr. Hoppy, who's the size of a three-year-old. Like always, she likes to go big. This keeps on getting better. Biting my lip to stop from laughing, I pick out a mouse Beanie Baby to take with me to school.

The minute I get to school, I rush into the bathroom and change out of my pajamas and into my regular clothes. Then I stuff my Beanie Baby into my backpack.

Of course, Hannah doesn't have a change of clothes. And she can't stuff that giant frog anywhere.

When I'm walking down the hallway after second period, I sense a tall, angry presence storming my way.

Hannah.

She's got a fluffy down coat on over her pajamas, and she's dragging around her giant frog. Her eyes chisel through me. "I can't reach my mom or your dad. I'm stuck like this for the *entire* day." As kids pass us, they stop and stare at Hannah in her bright blue Cookie Monster pajama bottoms that her parka definitely doesn't conceal.

"You could wear your gym clothes."

"That wouldn't be an improvement."

I shrug. "At least you have a coat."

A couple of sixth-grade girls stop to pet Hannah's frog.

"He's cute," one of them trills. "Can I take a selfie with him?"

"No!" snaps Hannah. The poor, terrified girl scurries away.

"I'm so sorry you're embarrassed," I say.

"I don't care what anyone thinks." Really? I know that she thinks she's a great actress, but she should stick to drawing because it's pretty obvious from her red face how she really feels. Tucking a strand of purple hair behind her ear, she glares at me. "Very soon you're going to really get it. It's going to be huge."

"Is that a threat?"

"Ohhhhh yeah." Whirling around, she whisks down the hall as everyone stares.

Oh boy.

I'm going to have to be prepared. Very.

Chapter Fourteen
ROLES TO PLAY

During the meeting of the Haunted House committee after school, I keep on waiting for the prank.

The huge prank.

Will she pull a chair away from me?

Or put whipped cream on my seat?

Maybe spill something? Spray something?

Write *Lily Loves Ethan* on a giant banner.

Draw a caricature of me as a lovesick elf?

The possibilities are endless and terrifying.

We're in our usual spot in the library, only Ms. Petrie is there to see how things are going. She's wearing boots with super-high heels. I have no idea how she can walk in them. This afternoon, I have the boxes of props with me. I have finished going through and now have a complete list of all the props and supplies contained in the box. Reese, Hannah, and some of the other members of the committee think I'm too uptight. But I'm proud of myself for learning a new program, and I can't wait to distribute the lists I made at our meeting today.

When I'm organized, I feel way more relaxed. On the other hand, Hannah keeps fidgeting with her ponytail. She's probably nervous to have to run the meeting with Ms. Petrie standing right there. Plus, she's still in her pajamas.

Hannah says we're going to all tell Ms. Petrie what parts we're playing. I bet Hannah is making us give updates because she hasn't written anything down and can't remember it all. It's so obvious.

Thanh Ha says she'll be a zombie who will "attack" and turn Lindsay into a zombie as well. The sixth-grade boys are going to be skeletons who pop out from behind headstones. Luke will saw Jonah in half, and the last part of the Haunted House will feature Reese as a demented clown, offering body parts to me, since I'm going to be a witch, making a crazy scary brew. And then, of course, Hannah and Ethan will be the stylish vampire guides.

"Great variety," declares Ms. Petrie. "Just know that we can't use a real chain saw or even a hacksaw."

Jonah and Luke moan in disappointment, but Ms. Petrie explains that it would be too much of a liability for the school in case someone was injured in the Haunted House. As if they would actually bring a real chain saw. Then again . . .

"By next week, I'd like all of you to write out the lines you're going to say and to start rehearsing them," she continues. "That means memorizing lines."

In my planner, I write down everything Ms. Petrie says in my note section. I peel off a silver sticker and place it next to my notes. That means that it's something that I need to worry about. Even though I'll just be saying just a few lines, I want to get them right.

Jonah rolls his eyes. "Can't I just improvise?"

"Yeah, c'mon," says Reese. "If we can't have a chain saw, can we at least make stuff up?" He eyes Hannah's pajamas. "You know, like *I want cookies*?"

A bunch of kids laugh but I'm actually not that happy.

There's no way I'm making anything up on the

spot. I'm definitely the sort of person who needs to know in advance what I'm going to do and say. I actually don't hate public speaking, as long as I have lines. That's the opposite of Keisha, who doesn't like to be in front of people. Well, unless she's on the ice, that is.

"I think that, in this case, improvising isn't a good idea," says Ms. Petrie. "We want all of our customers to have the same scare experience. However, if you all are interested in learning more about improvisation, maybe we could start a comedy improv troupe after school."

Some of the kids nod and give thumbs-up.

Okay, that's probably the last thing I'd want to do.

"Hey," says one of the sixth graders, "since we're skeletons who scare people, we don't have to memorize lines."

"Well, you still might want to agree on what you're going to say when you scare," explains Lindsay. "It could be *booooo*, or it could be something else."

Ms. Petrie glances at her clipboard. "So everyone will need to come up with a few lines. Oh, and especially Hannah and Ethan, since they will be our tour guides. It will be fun that our hosts will be dressed up like Dracula."

"Maybe Hannah and Ethan could get attacked," says Samir. "Thanh Ha and Lindsay could turn them into zombie vampires."

Ms. Petrie smiles. "Now that would be unexpected. But I'd rather we keep our guides out of the drama so that they can lead our guests safely out of the Haunted House."

I'm glad that I'm not going through the Haunted House this year as a regular person. I hate surprises.

"We'll have groups of up to eight people come through at a time," explains Ms. Petrie. "When one group has gone through, we'll have a parent volunteer at the front to let the next group go through. That means Hannah will need to be also hooked up to a walkie-talkie so she can communicate and let the parents know when a group is all the way through."

I raise my hand. "That would be right after I've made everyone touch the brew full of eyeballs—which will be grapes—and the intestines, which will be spaghetti."

"That sounds perfect," says Ms. Petrie.

After she leaves, Hannah says we should all work on figuring out our scripts today, while the sixth graders can start deciding what they want to write on the gravestones.

For a few moments, I'm sitting by myself peacefully. But it's not quiet for long, though. Reese and Luke literally hop up onto my table. They sit next to each other, dangling their legs.

"So do you think Luke should use a plastic ax or would it better to use a plastic saw?" asks Reese.

"Um, what's scarier?" I say.

Popping up behind them, Jonah pushes Luke and Reese. "This!" They fall forward, stumbling onto the carpet.

Once Reese steadies himself, he heads over to Jonah and shoves him. "Thanks a lot," he grumbles.

Jonah punches Reese on the arm, and I can tell it hurts because he winces. Before it had been playful, but this is something different.

"What the heck?" says Reese.

"Wow," says Luke, like Jonah is really crazy.

Jonah shakes his head. "If I'm crazy, then you're a lunatic."

Reese stalks away to sit by himself. But about five minutes later, he and Jonah are sitting together again and smiling.

I don't understand Reese at all. How could he just forget? Like right now he and Jonah are laughing because Luke just fell for a prank voicemail saying that he was going to be arrested for streaking.

Before the meeting ends, I pull out some of the props to show everyone. There are some really cool rubbery bugs, fake spiderweb stuff, and even talking skulls that just need batteries. "I figured out that we have plenty of black cloth to hang up on the walls. It's all in one of the prop boxes. So we don't need to buy that. Plus, we have plenty of leftover plastic fangs, which gives us enough money in our budget to buy something else."

Reese leans back in his chair. "Remember how I said that you were going too far with all the lists and organization? Well, I take that back—it was a good idea."

"Ha!" I say. "See, being organized isn't geeky."

"Yep," agrees Reese. "Now we have plenty of money to buy candy!"

When the meeting is over, I stuff all of the prizes and props back into the boxes.

Reese stays and helps me, which I didn't expect since all of his friends left right away.

"How come you're still talking to Jonah?" I blurt out before I can stop myself.

He gives me a blank stare as if I'm asking how he knows how to walk.

"Earlier. He punched you."

"Oh yeah." He shrugs.

"How can you just forget?"

"He's my friend, so I just do."

"Were you always that way? Mr. Forgiving?"

He tosses some plastic fingernails into the box. "Nah. In kindergarten, Jonah used to kick my sand-castles. And I used to cry. Then I avoided him. Then I figured out that sometimes you have to let it go. I mean, you can't let people walk all over you, but you can't hold grudges either." He taps his forehead. "It also helps I have a short memory." He gets up to leave and so do I.

It's weird how Reese is so easy to talk to, the way that Keisha is. Seventh grade is definitely not starting out like I expected. Everything feels upside down. And scary!

Chapter Fifteen
PRACTICE MAKES PERFECT

I'm in the kitchen making a practice piecrust. I want to figure out how to do the lattice kind, because I think they look extra pretty. Plus, you can see exactly what kind of filling you're getting. It's not easy. The strips of dough have to be exactly the same size. They can't be too thick and they can't be too thin.

I go back into my room to get my phone to look up advice on making dough strips. When I walk over to my bed, I gasp. The contents of my backpack have been spilled onto the floor—again. Granola bar wrappers, gum, permission slips, textbooks.

Hannah!

"I can't believe you went through my backpack again," I say, storming back into the living room. "And threw my stuff all over the room!"

"But I didn't," insists Hannah.

"Right. Just like it was a happy accident you put food dye in my toothpaste on picture day. Just like you're forcing my dad to agree to drive you into Seattle to go to GeekGirlCon in a few weeks, when you know that, so far, he hasn't had time to go apple picking with me."

"He's taking you apple picking this Saturday."

"Whatever. You're just trying to hog him, like you hog everything."

"You're so delusional. About everything. Anyway, your dad volunteered."

"More like you made him."

Hannah heaves a dramatic sigh. She is always tossing herself and her junk into my life. And I'm now literally tripping right over it.

A couple of hours later, the laundry I had carefully folded earlier is strewn all over the bedroom.

Great. Hannah again.

I stomp into the living room to confront her about it. But she doesn't notice me. There's some random

Netflix show streaming on the TV and Hannah's glaring at a drawing on her iPad.

"What's the matter?" asks Dad, who's sitting across from her on a recliner. I'm absolutely shocked he's not asleep, because he was up super late last night working on an editing project.

Sucking in a breath, I prepare for Dad to take away our phones or even ground us since we've been fighting. But I see that he has earbuds in, and he's relaxing and listening to music.

Smiling, he pulls out his earbuds. "What's up, girls?"

Would Hannah tell him?

"I made the line on the elf's hair too dark," she moans.

Wow. Okay. She's not going to tell Dad.

"It's really important to make your lines light when you're doing the initial lay-in for a drawing," she continues.

As I stand there between them, my face feels warm and blotchy.

Of course, Dad doesn't ask why I'm standing there, clearly upset, but he does give me a kiss before he leaves to go to a photo shoot at a local high school football game.

As soon as he's out the door, I say to Hannah, "Somehow the laundry got mysteriously unfolded."

"Don't look at me."

Tapping my foot, I don't answer. I set my mouth in a tight line.

"Maybe you did it in your sleep," she says.

"That's crazy!" I exclaim loudly.

At that moment, Kimberly opens the door, home from work.

She sets down her bag, "What's crazy, Lily?"

"Nothing." I'm not about to accuse Hannah in front of Kimberly of dumping the laundry.

Not with everything else left to explain.

Kimberly glares at the television, the iPad, and then at Hannah. "What are you doing?"

Hannah shrugs. "Taking a break."

"And I'm trying to figure out crusts," I say. "I don't have any homework."

Kimberly looks toward the kitchen. "Lily, I'm so glad you're making use of all of those baking supplies."

"Yeah." What I don't say is that I've discovered I really don't like to bake by myself. It's a Mom-and-Lily thing. But I can't say that aloud.

Kimberly turns to Hannah. "You were supposed to be studying for your social studies test on Monday. How many times have I told you to do chores and homework before watching a show or messing around on your iPad?" She puts out her hand. "Hannah, phone please."

"What? I was about to study."

"It doesn't matter what you were about to do. Phone. Now. I'm just taking it away for today, but if you continue to procrastinate, it will be two days."

"Fine." Hannah gives up her cell.

"There's no Netflix right now, either. There's only studying for your test."

"Okaaaay." Hannah looks as if it's all my fault.

It's not. She's the one who needs to get more organized when it comes to schoolwork.

After dinner, Hannah is still not studying for her social studies test. And I'm finally done refolding laundry.

"I'm really looking forward to apple picking tomorrow morning," I say to Dad as he and Kimberly sip a glass of wine in the kitchen. "I can't believe the Fall Festival is just one week from today."

"About that." He looks at Kimberly. Kimberly looks

at him. "On Saturday, there are two open houses that Michele says we can't miss." For a moment, I don't know who they are talking about, and then I remember that Michele is their realtor.

"I'm so sorry," says Dad.

"It's the sort of thing that, with this market, unless you put the first offer . . ." Kimberly's voice trails off.

"This whole house-hunting thing's crazy," says Dad. "But it'll pay off. We'll soon have the home we always wanted."

"Okay," I say. But it's not okay. I would have said yes to going to Keisha's ice-skating competition tomorrow. Now it's too late, because her parents have already left since the competition is hours away.

"Next time can you give me a little warning?"

"Yes, definitely," says Dad. "I promise this will all be over soon."

After he gives me a hug, I go to my room. Actually, not my real room. I still feel like a guest here.

On Saturday morning, I'm thrilled that it's finally time to video chat with Mom. I miss her *so* much. She looks a little tired this time, because she's been fighting a cold. Otherwise, she tells me that things are going really well.

I can't say the same.

"Things are more amazing here than I thought possible," she confesses. "Colleagues at work are always inviting me to dinner at their homes. The entire family's there. When I say entire, I mean parents, even great-aunts and uncles sometimes. The food's incredible. At the last house I went to, there were some girls your age, and they reminded me of you."

"Except they are married," I say, trying to joke.

Mom frowns. "No, of course not. One girl was studying almost the entire time because she wants to go into bioengineering, and with all of her plans and lists she's so much like you. I think the two of you would get along."

"That's great," I say, and then I tell Mom more about Maisie. How I've been working with her on playing catch in the backyard.

"There are quite a few dogs around here," says Mom. "I can't quite tell which dog belongs to which family. It's very interesting, actually, this whole sense of community, and everyone taking care of everyone. The idea of family is so large. The one thing I'm adjusting to is a lack of privacy. I find that I'm hardly ever alone. It's so different from the US in that way."

"Not necessarily," I say. "I'm sharing a room."

"Well, that's good for you."

"You say it like it's medicine." I realize my voice sounds accusatory but I can't help it. "And, Mom, Hannah's a complete slob. I mean you've never in your life seen anything like it."

"*Essh*. I didn't realize."

"But don't worry. We're getting along," I hastily add because I promised myself I wouldn't have Mom worry about that part.

"Well, okay. I'm sure it's not easy having different living styles." *Understatement*, I think. "But it's good to learn how to deal with different kinds of people and situations," adds Mom.

"It's different all right." But unlike Mom traveling in Morocco, it's not different in a good way. "You don't even always speak the same language," I say, since Mom speaks French but only a little bit of Arabic. "And you're getting along perfectly. On the other hand, Hannah and I speak the same language, but we can't understand each other." There. I've said it. I've confessed a little bit to Mom that my stepsister and I are not exactly BFFs.

"You need to communicate then," says Mom patiently.

"But—"

"But nothing. It's vital."

"If I communicate, I'll say things I regret. Hannah's so sensitive."

"Then write her a note. Let her know exactly how you feel."

"Wow," I say. Why hadn't I thought of that? "I can do that!"

Chapter Sixteen
IT'S GOING DOWN

On Sunday morning, I write a note to Hannah.

Hannah,

From the second I arrived, you've been hostile. What's your problem? Other than the fact that you're rude and a slob? Do you think that I actually want to be in the same room as you either? It's not my fault my dad decided to marry your mom!

I'm sick and tired of everything about you, because it's all about you, isn't it? I know you go through my stuff. Well, it's stopping now.

I'm going to throw all of your stuff in the garbage where it belongs.

Lily

Wait! There's no way that I can send that. I rip it up, write a new letter, and slip it inside a book in my backpack. It says,

Dear Hannah.

STOP DIGGING IN MY BACKPACK!

The only way you could find this note would be to go through my stuff. Feel free to tell your mom and my dad. That way they'll know too. Please do it. I want you to.

Sincerely,

Lily

I place my backpack on the floor at the foot of my bed, and then I walk to the kitchen to get a snack. I can't wait for Hannah to discover my note. She's on the couch, sketching. I wait for her to head into our room. Only she's not moving.

It's like watching a pot that never boils.

So I decide to distract myself by practicing my flute. When I go back into my room, I see a mess. Wrappers from my backpack litter the floor, along with my notebooks and water bottle. Someone has clearly been rummaging through my backpack!

I go to accuse Hannah, but I remember she just left for swim practice. How convenient for her.

When I check the rest of the contents in my backpack, I see that the note I wrote to Hannah is still there. However, it's now smudged.

Wow! She's really even more of a slob than I thought. If I searched her stuff, I would put everything back exactly as I found it.

When I go to check my phone to text Keisha about this, my phone isn't in the side pocket of my backpack where I usually keep it. It's not in any of my pockets.

I can't believe Hannah would steal my phone!

I look everywhere for it. The floor. The couch. The kitchen table. The bathroom.

It's nowhere.

I want to text Hannah that this is way too low, but I can't because I don't have my phone!

It's one thing to prank and annoy me, but outright theft?! I guess this is her version of payback for Pajama Day.

What if Mom wants to chat with me? What if Keisha is texting me? Or even Reese to talk about the witch's brew?

"Where's my phone?" I scream in frustration, and Maisie trots over. She sniffs my hand. I can tell she's worried. "You didn't do anything wrong, Maisie. The other person who lives in this room did. In a big way."

That's when I decide it's time for me to go through Hannah's backpack. At the bottom of her pack, I retrieve her social studies textbook. She has a test Monday, but hasn't studied yet, which comes as no surprise, since she always crams.

Well, no more waiting until the last moment this time. I stuff the textbook into the very back of her closet, and it's immediately swallowed by mounds of clothes, papers, books, and shoes.

Maybe I shouldn't have hidden it that well. But I can't help that Hannah's side of the closet is such a junk pile. Serves her right for hiding my phone, since she knows how much I rely on it to check for texts from Mom.

After I'm done moping, I go and email Mom on the computer in the kitchen. I tell her how I'm starting to get nervous about the pie contest. I suggest that we bake the apple pie together via video chat. Well, more like her watching me bake. I also let Mom know more about the Fall Festival. I write:

The Haunted House has been a lot of work but also fun. Can't believe it's coming up next Friday!

The prop list is crazy: baby dolls to turn into zombies, rags that we can dye red, a sound effects tape with screams, moans, chains, heavy breathing, screech owls, and maniacal laughter. You should see the funny gravestones a few of the boys have been working on. Somehow they're funny and creepy at the same time. It will be part of a larger scary cemetery, where we have talking skulls that chatter and howl. We bought cobwebs that we'll string up everywhere, so it will look all spidery.

Next to my cauldron, I'll have dry ice so it will look like there's steam rising off the poisonous brew. We have a fog machine that will add to the atmosphere. Also, we're putting black sheets up on all the walls to keep things dark and spooky. Plus, we will use flickering lights to get everyone messed up. We're also going to make it cluttered and maze-like.

Just like Hannah's side of the room, but I don't say that part. But I definitely learned from her how to clutter things up!

On Monday morning, I start feeling guilty about my textbook prank. Maybe it's because, right before breakfast, I find my phone wedged between seat cushions on the couch.

Of course, I know Hannah hid my phone. I don't sit on that side of the couch, only she does. But still. Having my phone back makes feel a little less angry.

Nevertheless, right before we leave for school, I don't tell Hannah her textbook is sitting in the back of her closet. Not that she's looking.

When I get to school, I confess my guilt to Keisha, who doesn't make me feel worse about the textbook. Still, I know she hasn't exactly approved of our sister battle.

"I really shouldn't feel too bad," I say. "It's not as if Hannah didn't just hide my phone. And it's not exactly like she's been nice. Everything's *all* about her. She never stops to ask me about anything. Well, she does, at the very end of a conversation, right when she conveniently has to go."

"Yeah, well, some people are like that," says Keisha. "It's all about them."

"People like Hannah deserve to learn a lesson." At least, that's what I tell myself. And Hannah really does do all her schoolwork last minute, which accounts for her uneven grades. She crams for her tests and quizzes and gets anywhere from a D to an A. All of her papers are written the night before, and yet, somehow, she stills manages to pull off a B range or even an A-minus sometimes.

During pre-algebra, Luke brags that he beat Keisha doing our timed problem sets.

"I'm done!" Luke yells out.

I wasn't even close to finishing.

"Do you have to yell it out?" says Keisha. "And you were barely first, Luke. I just finished seconds after you."

"Actually," says Luke. "I *do* need to shout it out. Because you're slow, and I'm not."

"I am *not* slow," declares Keisha, who's a math whiz, in addition to be an ice-skating whiz. "And not only was I fast, but I bet I was more accurate than you."

I give Keisha a high five. "Nice one!"

For the rest of the day, Luke's boasting gets to me. Why do some people have to put other people down to feel good about themselves?

When I'm walking to social studies, I ask Reese about it.

"In math, Luke can be such a jerk. He's always boasting. He's your friend. Can you please explain?"

"He needs self-certification," says Reese.

"What? I've never hard of that."

"I mean, self-validation. He just needs it. It has nothing to do with any of us."

"Really? He seems so confident."

"My mom's a therapist, and she says that whatever people say, it's usually all about them. If they call you something, it's because they're feeling that way. And if someone's truly confident, they don't need validation."

That made me think about Hannah. Sometimes she's so frustrated with her art. Other times, she compliments herself. Was she secretly super insecure and just needs validation? It was hard to believe but possible.

What is even harder to believe is that the Fall Festival is now just four days away! This Friday! After school, my committee meets in the gym, and we begin to construct the Haunted House inside of a huge supply closet that's the size of classroom. It's filled with cones, balls, Hula-Hoops, and other gym stuff, leaving the rest of the space vacant. This allows us to construct temporary walls using the school's supply of rolling whiteboards, which we cover with black cloth and tarps. After creating a maze of rooms, we will fill the various spaces with creepy props. It's tricky taping down all of the cords to the various chattering skulls, so nobody trips, as well as the cord to the sound system.

When I get home from school, I watch a couple of videos from Ethan's YouTube channel, and they're surprisingly cringe-y. They're mostly him playing some video game while he loudly crunches on chips, saying how awesome he's doing. I switch to watching videos on baking pies. I want to watch the experts, to see if there's anything else that I can learn. I'm surprised at how much Mom has taught me. One baker says it's really important to buy fresh organic fruit, while another says it's all about the art of the crust. Right now, since I can't get Dad to take me to the orchard, I'm going to have to get my apples from the grocery store. Still, they have really good apples in Tacoma, and they're often trucked in fresh that day.

After I do some language arts reading, I go to the living room to work on teaching Maisie how to sit and to stay. This is only after I watched some dog training videos, which were super helpful.

When Hannah comes into the room, she doesn't say a word to me about her textbook or her test. Instead, she says, "It's time for Maisie to spend some time with me." Then she proceeds to give Maisie a treat, even though she didn't do anything to deserve it.

"You're spoiling her," I say.

"I'm being nice."

"Nice? What do you know about that?" I realize my voice is raising. "All you know is disorganization and chaos!"

"And what do you know about being non-judgmental? Little Miss Perfect!"

"Girls, you need to dial it back right now," says Dad from the kitchen.

"Absolutely," says Kimberly. "I won't stand for screaming."

I wait for them to follow through on some kind of punishment.

A chair scrapes on the floor. It's not like I can say anything about my phone, not when I hid Hannah's textbook.

"Lily, I think you need some time off in your room," says Dad.

Reluctantly, I plod to the bedroom and sink down into my bed. Right now, I just feel like a bad apple.

In my room, I think about my words to Hannah—about her being disorganized. That was one of my Mom's main beefs with my dad. That he wasn't responsible and just flitted from one thing to another because of his lack of his ability to live his life to a schedule or have any organization. Some of it was true and some of it was harsh because my dad is creative and a dreamer. I remember one really bad argument involving door slamming and Mom cracking some clay pot Dad had just made.

My throat aches at the memory. Mom was taking all of these classes, which we couldn't afford. Plus, Dad had just lost his sales job. At that point, he hadn't had a job in almost four months, and he was taking a ceramics class instead of having a "real job," so it was bad.

Now Dad has his own video business, and a new wife, so it's different. But still. Between work and house hunting, he doesn't have time for anything else, like apple picking or noticing that his stepdaughter is passive-aggressive, or more like just plain aggressive.

It wasn't a good thing to tell Hannah she was completely disorganized. Dad definitely took it the wrong way.

And it's really weird how she didn't mention her social studies test. In fact, she was strangely silent about it, which makes me nervous.

What could she possibly be planning next?

Chapter Seventeen
HOW 'BOUT THEM APPLES

After school on Wednesday, I start to freak out. The Fall Festival is happening in two days.

Two!

Not only are there posters up all over the school, but talk of it is all over the neighborhood. I noticed that they wrote a story about it in our neighborhood newspaper. They probably do it every year, but I'm definitely more aware of anything to do with the Fall Festival now that I'm a part of it.

Every time I see a poster about the pie contest, my chest tightens. I want to finally win at something. Keisha has all of her ribbons and trophies from skating. Even for a math competition that she won in sixth grade. And Hannah has her swim trophies and her first-place ribbons for art.

I would like to be excellent at something, too.

Just one ribbon. One real ribbon, not just an honorable mention or participation ribbon.

As I sit down at my desk in my room to do some homework, I get a text from Keisha, which is surprising since she's usually on the ice at this hour.

Keisha: *I miss you xoxo* she texts me.

Me: *Me too!*

Keisha: *I'm done with skating practice early. Come over? I've got news!*

Me: *I can't. I've got to wait until my dad comes home so he can take me shopping for pie ingredients.*

Keisha: *Don't wait. We can shop together!*

Me: *Really?*

Keisha: *Yes, I'd totally go food shopping with you.*

On our bikes, we meet at the local grocery store that I absolutely love. They keep produce in these really cool wooden crates that make the place look like a farmers market. And best of all, they have all of these varieties of locally grown apples; it's almost as good as buying them from the orchard.

Even dressed in her sweats and fresh from a hard workout at the rink, Keisha looks great. Her curly hair is pulled back with a wide purple headband. She gives me a hug and she's grinning.

"Okay, why are you smiling?" I ask. "Your braces were tightened yesterday. You shouldn't be so happy. Plus, you should be tired."

"I figured out my music for my new routine."

"That's awesome!" I say, as we start to inspect the apples. The Braeburns look so shiny. But I'm always dubious of shiny apples. Mom says that they shine them up when they're not quite as good as they should be. "So what song did you finally pick for your new routine?"

"This new song by Rihanna that I absolutely love." Her voice sounds excited.

"Can you do that?"

"My coach was totally on board!"

"That's awesome."

"Hey, do you want to hang tomorrow after we finish festival committee stuff? I'm not going to skating practice."

"I wish. I've got to run home to video chat and bake with my mom."

"Wow. That means she'll be staying up really late."

"I know. It'll be about 11:30 for her if we start at 3:30." Although I'm tempted by some Jonagolds, I stick to my usual—locally grown Granny Smiths and Honeycrisps. They're not cheap, which is why we only shop here for specialty items.

I figure buying pricey apples for the perfect apple pie is worth it. Dad gave me extra money for my allowance this week.

I'm so happy, I buy chocolate chip cookies and two bottles of apple cider.

"You really can buy my heart with anything chocolate," says Keisha.

"I know." We sit on the curb and devour our cookies and drink the ridiculously sweet cider. Rain patters on the roof and we laugh as water slides down our cheeks.

"Oh, by the way, Quinn asked me if I wanted to meet him at this coffee shop on Saturday."

"Excuse me? You're just now telling me? *The* Quinn who you've been crushing on for six months asked you out?"

"It's not a date. We have a skating thing, and he said we should meet up at this coffee shop afterwards for doughnuts."

"That is *so* a date. Did he invite your friends?"

"No." Keisha giggles. "Okay. Okay, it's a quasi date but don't spook me. If I make too big a deal about it, I won't be able to skate well."

"So it's just a completely minor thing that a very cute guy wants to hang with you and eat doughnuts."

"Exactly. No biggie."

"If Ethan asked me to do something like that, I'd faint."

"Who's fainting?" says a familiar voice. Ugh! It's Hannah. And not just Hannah but it's also Thanh Ha and Lindsay. They're locking up their bikes right next to us.

Great. I might as well have gotten on the loud-speaker at school.

"So what are you guys doing here?" I realize I sound like an idiot.

"The same thing as you," says Thanh Ha. She smiles at me and so does Lindsay. "Getting something good to eat!"

Like Lindsay and Hannah, she's wearing a rain jacket, even though honestly it's hardly doing anything but drizzling. I had no idea that the three of them hung out together outside of the Haunted House committee. Then again, come to think of it, Hannah's so overscheduled, she rarely has time to hang with anyone.

Wait a minute? What is Hannah doing here? "Are you supposed to be at swim practice?" I say.

She snaps her lock shut. "Have you memorized my schedule?" Rolling her eyes, she glances over at Lindsday and Thanh Ha as if I'm some sort of organizational freak, which I am, but that's beside the point.

Actually, while I haven't exactly memorized Hannah's schedule, I've recently written it down in my planner. That way I'll pretty much know when Hannah will be gone and can enjoy a few minutes of peace. "We've lived together for almost a month, so yeah, I do kind of know your schedule, I guess."

"That's so weird," announces Hannah. Thanh Ha and Lindsay stare at the pavement like this all is embarrassing them. "It's raining," continues Hannah. "Why are you sitting on the curb?"

"Because we want to!" says Keisha. Oh, I love my best friend!

"We're living like the mountain is out," I say, or at least I'm trying live that way. Thanks to Keisha.

"Lily, do you do anything besides obsess over schedules and apples?" Hannah sneers as she moves to follow Thanh Ha and Lindsay into the store.

"Hannah, maybe I should take a photo of you here," I say, pulling out my phone and opening the camera app.

She stops in her tracks.

Now it's my turn to smile as I point the phone at her. "And I can post it on Snappypic. I'm sure your mom wouldn't care that you're not at swim practice. After all, you're already going to the OOs"

"JOs," she corrects me.

Hannah jerks forward like she's going to snatch my phone out of my hands.

Then I do it—I take the photo, with flash.

She can't be nice to me for one second. She totally deserves this!

"You better not post that photo," she says hotly, and then the door swings shut behind her.

"You can't tell me what to do!" I shout.

Only she's inside with her friends and can't hear me.

"You really shouldn't post that photo," says Keisha. "But if you did, I could totally understand why. I know she's having you be the witch and all for the Haunted House. But honestly, she could just play herself and scare plenty of people. She doesn't even need any green face makeup."

"She scared you?" I'm shocked. Keisha is not scared of trying a double axel. Or crazy jumps. But Hannah? "Seriously? You're scared of *her*?'"

"She gets me all jittery inside. Like I've been on the rink too long."

I feel like dancing. Because I'm not crazy. Now Keisha actually sees what I'm talking about.

I post the photo and Kimberly sees it, and Hannah gets in big trouble.

She was supposed to be at swim practice. But she was skipping it.

So now Hannah's phone has been taken away for an entire week and she is giving me the silent treatment. I do feel a little bit guilty, but mostly I feel like Kimberly and my dad are starting to see that Hannah is not exactly perfect. Kimberly said that if Hannah crossed the line again, she was taking away GeekGirlCon.

By Thursday, the Haunted House is almost all set up! It's so spooky and really cool-looking. Immediately, when you first enter, the gravestones create a creepy atmosphere. But they are also a little funny. One says say REST IN PIECES with a grim reaper hovering right over the stone. Two others say AL. B. BACK and BERRY D. HATCHET.

Spider webs drip from the black-covered walls. Test tubes and odd body parts lay scattered atop tables in the mad scientist's lab. Blinking lights in the zombie section make everything look weird and scary. Red paint splattered on all of the sheets looks like dripping blood. In my witch's lair, there are glass jars with creepy-looking ingredients like bugs, tongues, and eyeballs. With the fog machine, dry ice, and sound effects, the atmosphere is complete.

The entire committee are in their costumes, and now it's time to rehearse, since other than before we open tomorrow, we won't have much time.

A sheet is draped over Jonah's head, and he's carrying a rubber mask on a tray. "Don't you think it's pretty realistic?" he asks.

"It does, especially since it's dark in here," I admit. We are keeping the Haunted House as gloomy as possible, only a few lamps here and there to create an eerie glow, so people can find their way through the rooms.

Jonah lifts the tray with the severed plastic head up into the air.

"Not pretty," I say, pretend wincing. Jonah found red tubes that look like arteries and veins, so the head is especially gross.

"Hey, I got it." Reese snaps his fingers. "Jonah, you should drop the head. Then splash it into a bucket of water with red flood coloring."

Thanh Ha folds her arms. "No way. It'll get on people's clothes."

"So what?" Samir shrugs. "People should enter the Haunted House at their own risk."

"Yeah," says Reese. "We even have a sign in the front that says that."

"Which I painted," adds Samir. "Thank you very much."

"How about if it's just water?" I suggest.

"Drop the head!" the sixth graders chant. And, somehow, we agree at the very last minute to create a scene where Jonah drops his own head after Luke saws it off.

I'm not a fan of doing anything at the last minute, but everyone seems to think it won't add that much time to the experience, since Ms. Petrie wants to make sure customers don't have to wait in line too long.

Suddenly, I notice something: Reese isn't in his clown costume. Instead, he's wearing white painter's pants covered in dirty-looking white strips.

"Is that your clown outfit?" I ask, confused.

"Nope," says Reese. "Hold that thought. I'll be right back."

When he returns about five minutes later, he's dressed like a mummy. "A mummy!" I exclaim. "That wasn't in the plans."

"True!" Reese grins. At least, I think he's grinning. It's hard to know what he's doing beneath his bandages.

Spinning around, I see why Reese's pants are covered in ripped-up, dirty white strips. "I soaked the strips in coffee water first. Nice touch, right?"

"Um, yeah."

He kicks out his feet, showing off his masking tape-covered boots. "Tada! Mummy boots! As I move around, the severed eyeballs move around with me. Because they're duct-taped to the outside of the bandages, where my forehead is. Like it?"

"Sure." What I can't understand is how Reese can possibly see. But there do appear to be slits in his bandages somewhere near his actual eyes. "It's definitely original."

"That's the point. I don't want to be some cheesy, typical mummy."

"Don't worry, Reese. You're not typical. I don't even understand how you're talking right now."

"It's called a mouth. And it still works."

"I thought you were going to be a clown."

"You're right. But I got inspired. Actually, I'm ripped up about it!" Then he somehow rips off his entire mummy outfit. Underneath is a clown suit, complete with fluffy puff-ball buttons and a red ball nose.

"Wow!" I say. "That's, um, surprising." My phone pings, and I look down. It's a text from my mom.

So sorry, honey. I can't chat and bake the pie with you after school because of a last-minute work trip. I won't have wifi. We'll definitely take a rain check. And in Washington that won't be hard ☺

I type back: *Mom, please. I need you. It's for the contest tomorrow.*

She responds: *I really wish I could, babu. I can't. Sending hugs! xoxo*

"See, underneath I'm a demented clown," Reese is saying. "Freaky, right?" He pauses. "Hey, you're still not smiling. Or listening. Is something wrong?"

"It's nothing." I shrug.

"It's not nothing. Tell me."

I pause. Should I tell Reese? "My mom's on a fellowship in Morocco. And we were supposed to bake an apple pie together. After school, actually, when it would be crazy late for her. Only now, she can't because of some work/travel thing."

"Sorry for being clueless, but how could you bake a pie together, if she's over there and you're here? Isn't there, like, a continent and an ocean between here and, um, Africa?"

"Well, there's video chat."

"Oh, right. You were going to bake, and she was going to watch."

"Exactly. I'm now going to have to bake all by myself. Which sucks. I wish so badly she were here. Plus, she's going to miss the whole festival. All of it."

"Even me?" He taps his demented-clown, pom-pom chest.

"Yup, even you. She'd think you're funny and really like your crazy outfit." I can't believe I'm saying this.

"I can film this," he says, gesturing to the room. "You know, the Haunted House, for her."

"How? You're in the Haunted House. You're a mummy, Reese. Well, a mummy clown."

"I'll just ask one of my friends to film it on their phone for us. Then, voilà, put it up on YouTube."

"That'd be amazing! Thanks." I pause. "That's really nice of you."

"Don't tell anyone, Magic. It'd ruin my reputation."

I sigh. "Will you ever tell me why you call me Magic?"

"Do you really want to know?"

"Um, yes. I've been asking you forever."

"I'll tell you at the festival. During one of our breaks."

"Hm, okay."

When I go back to hanging up a skeleton, I see, out of the corner of my eye, Reese write *hi* in orange ink on Jonah's backpack.

I stare at him in surprise. "It was you, wasn't it? Who wrote on my backpack a few weeks ago?"

"Nope." His ears turn carnation pink.

"Look, I'm not going to tell on you. I'm not going to get mad. Just tell me the truth. Did you draw *hi* on my backpack a few weeks ago?"

"You expect me to remember that long ago?"

"Uh-huh."

"I might have."

He's blushing. Why is Reese blushing? Could he be embarrassed?

Later, as I walk home with Keisha, I tell her about the backpack incident. "Reese admitted he wrote on my backpack and he was blushing. Isn't that weird?"

"He could be overheated. And he could be really embarrassed he got caught. I know I would be if Quinn caught me."

"But that's different. You . . ." I stumble on my words. "Like Quinn."

"Well, maybe Reese likes you."

"What? No. That's crazy."

"I'm not so sure about that."

"Reese is cute. But he's always being silly."

"So?" She doesn't wait for my response. "You should get him back. Write: *Hey, look what I did. Bwahahaha!* You could do it on his notebook. But you have to look out for teachers and tattletales. But you don't like him now that he may like you, do you?"

"What? No. No way!"

"Good because you never write on a boy's notebook that you actually like because you could accidentally get carried away. You know, like start drawing hearts and lose track of the time and then he might catch you."

"I wouldn't do that."

"Good. I'm just checking. You never can be sure."

Before I start to bake that evening, I read an email from Mom offering tips. Most of them I know by heart, but it still feels good to receive the advice.

Give the apple slices enough time to drain.

Don't use too many super sweet apples. Stay balanced.

Be generous when you flour your rolling pin.

Keep the fluting even.

Take your time.

Slice the apples with love.

Mom always says that food can tell when you're in a bad mood. Food wants you to be happy.

I try very hard to be happy, even though I miss Mom, but I try not to think too hard about it. I use both Granny Smith and Honeycrisp apples, a perfect balance between tart and sweet. I make the slices thin, but not too thin.

And guess what? I'm in a pretty good mood, and, shockingly, so is Hannah. She has her drawing all ready to go for the art contest, and it looks amazing. There are so many details in the elf's clothing, even in the grass beneath her feet. I tell her that I'm sure she's going to win, and she says that my pie, which is cooling, looks really good, which shocks me.

You can tell that the texture of the crust is going to be flaky, without tasting too papery, and that it will be buttery, without being too rich. The whole room smells wonderful. Hannah says so. And Dad and Kimberly, too.

Before I go to bed, I listen to binaural beats to get myself calm enough to actually go to sleep. And I read Mom's email all over again. Starting with the apple pie advice. She finishes with:

So take your time with the apples, just remember to have fun. It's going to be delicious.

Then she goes on to to let me know about her latest insights about Morocco.

When I come back home, we should take off our shoes inside the apartment. It's a thing here that I like. Once inside, everyone puts on slippers. It makes so much sense. It keeps the floors cleaner, and it's more comfortable.

By the way, I'm meeting so many people. I asked this older couple directions, and they invited me over and served mint tea, very sweet and delicious. Tomorrow night, I'm going over there for dinner.

Can you imagine? Random strangers inviting me into their home? It's all about trust. I think we all just need to open up and let the world know we're ready.

Okay, I tell the world—*I'm ready. Very ready!*

Chapter Eighteen
ALMOST SHOWTIME

On Friday morning, I hear Kimberly call out, "You girls up?"

"Yes!" I say. Because it's not just any Friday. It's *the* Friday. It's the day of the Fall Festival. It's the day that we are going to have the most amazing Haunted House ever, and Mom and I are going to get a blue ribbon for our pie. Well, my pie, but only technically. Even though I don't like admitting it, Hannah will probably win first place for her artwork. Again.

But it's seriously good.

My index finger brushes my phone. There was no waaaaaaay I could sleep in. I've been tossing and turning.

"Still waking up," Hannah croaks, wiping the sleep from her eyes.

"I'm showering," I announce, bouncing out of bed.

"Go ahead. I'm still waking up."

Hannah's still being nice? I'm going to pinch myself.

Later, after I'm all showered, I stride down the hall past all of the framed school photos of Hannah since kindergarten. Even back then, her hands were ink-splashed.

"Ready for the Fall Festival tonight?" I ask her.

"Oh yeah." Hannah gives me a thumbs-up.

I imagine the countless tables laden with all the pies in the exhibit hall, the lines of people waiting for the Haunted House. I can hear my name being announced as the winner of the pie contest and can see my blue first-place ribbon!

In the kitchen, there's a bowl of granola with almond milk for me at the table. I sit down, take a spoonful, but stop when I see that Dad's pacing.

"Is your pie okay?" he asks. "I don't see it."

"Oh, the pie. Don't worry, Dad." I skip over to the fridge and open the door. "It's here. Tada!" I point to it. The fluting came out better than I expected. This time when I crimped the edges, I was careful to consistently rotate the pie plate. Also, I made sure that dough was nice and chilled to keep its shape. Watching people make crust on YouTube really helped.

"So the pie was left at room temperature," I explain to Dad. "And it's been in the fridge overnight. Before you bring it over this afternoon, please keep it in the fridge. I'm hoping the judges don't taste it right away because the pie needs to be at room temperature. I'm little worried, since Mom says it can get warm inside the hall. Everyone swarms the gym to check out the pies."

"It will all work out," says Dad.

"I hope so!" Plopping back down in my chair, I eat my granola and a hard-boiled egg that I had cooked the night before. Got to fuel up for the big day ahead!

"Good luck with the contest today," says Dad. "Not that you'll need luck. The smells in the kitchen reminded me of the pies your mother used to make, and they were always delicious."

Wow. Dad paying Mom an actual compliment?

"I just wanted to wait until Kimberly had left before saying that," says Dad. "Since, you know . . ."

"I do. Kimberly's very nice, Dad."

"I think so, too." He gives me a kiss on my cheek. "I'm proud of you for working so hard on your committee and, of course, the pie. I know all of this change is not easy, especially with your mom being so far away. But the pie tasted amazing."

"What? How do you know?"

"I, well, did manage to taste a bit of the innards that gushed out through the slits." He pats his belly and I shake my head but give him a small laugh. "It's all going to be good. The Haunted House will be very busy and make a lot of money for the school."

"Thanks, Dad." I hug him, and he hugs me back.

Before I leave for school, I quickly video chat with Mom on my phone.

"I'm wishing you luck on the contest," she says. "I know the judges will love your pie."

"Our pie," I correct. "But thanks. The Haunted House is going to be awesome, too. I have all my lines memorized." I tell her about Reese, and how, at the last minute, he decided to not just be a crazy clown but also a mummy, who strips off his bandages and becomes a clown.

"I'm not quite sure I understand."

"I'm not sure I do, either. You have to see it to believe it. And, luckily, we're going to film the Haunted House today! Reese's asking some friends of his to film it. Hopefully, they'll squeal in terror and stuff. Which I think they will. Everyone's doing a great job, and I have to admit Hannah's found some pretty creepy costumes, including the vampire outfits she and Ethan will be wearing."

"I never thought I'd say this," says Mom, "but that all sounds wonderful! I had worried at first that maybe you and Hannah weren't exactly getting along. But then you never said anything about it. Though your dad filled me in a little a bit. He admitted that there's be some hiccups, but he said it was normal transition stuff. He was a little concerned."

"Yeah, well, I didn't quite know he was concerned." Or that Mom knew about the hiccups all along. So I may as well let her in now. "Okay, it's been way more than hiccups. I was hoping nobody noticed. I wanted to take care of things myself. I was trying to remain calm even when she was making me angry."

"Well, let's just say your father and Kimberly were both watching, and I've been telling them that these things take time. People need to adjust." She pauses. "Why didn't you tell me, Lily?"

"Well, you also weren't asking me about it."

"I guess you weren't giving me specifics and I didn't want to push."

"I didn't want you to be upset. I wanted you to be proud of how well I was doing."

"You never need to hide things from me."

"I wanted to keep my promise," I say in a quiet voice.

"I said to try to get along. I didn't say to pretend to get along. I value honestly above all else. But it must be honesty married to compassion and kindness."

It's ironic to hear Mom use the word *married*, given her situation. "Yes," I say. "I'll try all that."

"I know your stepmom is thrilled that things are going in this direction." How could Mom say, *my step-mom*? She, of all people. Originally, I had refused to call Kimberly my stepmom to other people. It sounded too close to the word *mom*. I would never say, for example, *I'm going my dad and stepmom's*. Instead, I'd say, *My dad and Kimberly's*. Even Kimberly never referred to herself as my stepmom. After the wedding, she just said for me to call her Kimberly. Hannah, on the other hand, often publicly calls my dad her step-dad. I've heard her on the phone with her friends say, "Gotta go, my stepdad's coming."

But now my mom was doing it? Does she think of Kimberly as her replacement?

"Haven't you always wanted a sister?" gushes Mom.

"That's true." But I'm still not so sure about this situation.

Mom was humming. She only does that when she's happy. Really, *really* happy. And it's making me a little annoyed.

My mother is truly atom-splitting happy, and Kimberly and Dad are excited with the possibility of Hannah and me finally getting along. Even Hannah's been nicer than normal these last two days—and I got her in trouble! So, what's wrong with me?

Chapter Nineteen
That's the Way the Cookies Crumble

After school, my committee works on the finishing details of the Haunted House. Honestly, there's not much left to do. Just re-taping, securing props, and adding some black streamers for customers to walk through. It's only a little bit past noon, since today's a half day at school. That gives us about five hours until the festival starts. Everyone's super busy.

For a little bit, I leave the Haunted House to check what else is happening.

It's a drizzly afternoon but not rainy enough to cancel anything. Outside on the blacktop, kids and some teachers assemble the dunking booth, as well as all of the carnival games. Inside the gym, the artwork for the contest has been assembled and hung up on the walls. I pass by Hannah's elf drawing, and note that it's really one of the best sketches. Okay, there's really no doubt she will get another ribbon. Probably a blue one.

I stroll up and down the rows of empty tables, where the pie contest will be held. All the entry forms have been set up, so there's a spot just for my pie. An entry form has my name and grade on it, and soon enough Dad will place my pie right here:

Lily Silvers, Apple Pie Contestant, 7th grade.

Then I'll be able to breathe in the smell of pie, all that sweet and tangy fruit, and those flaky, buttery crusts. My mouth waters just thinking about it. In the late afternoon, the pies will arrive. Dad promised me that he would bring mine promptly at 5:00 p.m.

For a moment, I close my eyes and visualize my blue ribbon. I know exactly where I will put it up, right above my dresser, and when the wind blows through the window, it will flap pleasantly in the breeze, reminding me of this day.

As I head back to the Haunted House, I'm smiling. I may have never received a ribbon before, but today, maybe, it's a real possibility.

Suddenly Keisha races up to me. She seems out of breath.

"What's the matter?" I ask.

"The desserts are disappearing." She points to the section of the gym where she and a couple of others on the Refreshment committee are in charge of the cakewalk. "We set up the tables and put out all the cakes and stuff. Only, when we went to a closet to get more tables, half the brownies were missing!"

"Oh no, that's not good." I couldn't imagine how I would feel if something should happen to my pie.

"Luckily, it was just the brownies on one platter, but still. We need to wait to put out the other desserts. Otherwise, what if they all start to disappear? We won't have anything for the cakewalk."

"You could hide them," I suggest.

"Yes, we should. Totally." Keisha scans the various stations in the gym. "But where?"

"The Haunted House. In my witch's den. I have tables with black tablecloths. Just put everything under there until it's time to start the festival."

"Yes! Perfect! You're such a lifesaver." Keisha hugs me and we do our twirly thing.

"I try."

Soon, I'm helping Keisha carry trays of cakes into my witch's den. Reese and Jonah also volunteer to help.

"No eating any desserts," warns Keisha.

"Just one bite?" pleads Jonah, staring at the tray of wonder bars smothered in chocolate chips and coconut.

"Absolutely not," says Keisha. "We need them all as prizes."

"Next time we have a Haunted House, we should make blood brownies," suggests Reese. He's carrying a tray of sugar cookies shaped like pumpkins and a plate of cupcakes with fudge frosting sprinkled with M&M's.

"Gross," I say, as we walk into the back of the Haunted House.

"Not real blood." Reese laughs. "Just red-colored water."

With teamwork, it only takes five minutes to grab all the desserts and store them under the tables. "I kind of feel like the wicked witch from Hansel and Gretel," I say with a laugh.

"You look like her, too," confesses Keisha. My face is green. Plus, I'm wearing a gray wig, and I even found a kit so I could apply warts on my chin.

I cackle loudly and, backing up, Keisha pretends to be scared.

"Good luck!" I call out as she races off toward the basketball court where kids are measuring out the tape for the cakewalk.

With a happy sigh, I survey my witch's den. It's really so perfect. A collection of old brooms lean in the corner, next to a heap of bones on the floor. And just for fun, there's a cute Beanie Baby cat.

I stir the vat of grossness in my cauldron—cold spaghetti and peeled grapes, which are supposed to be eyeballs. In front of the cauldron we'll have steam rising from dry ice.

Thanh Ha walks into the room. "You have the best job," she admits, "because after kids touch the stew, you get to hand out the gummy worms. I hope you don't scare too many little children, though."

"I hope she does," says Reese, who just strolled back into the witch's den. He's now fully dressed as a mummy. "Scaring little children is the best.

Especially babies. If they have candy, make sure you take it from them." He grins.

"What?" Thanh Ha looks truly frightened, even though she's the one dressed like a zombie in a shredded-looking tunic. She also has on white makeup with fake flesh wounds.

"He's just kidding," I say to Thanh Ha.

"I worry about Reese," she admits.

"For good reason," I say.

A few minutes later, I check my phone. "Oh, it's almost time for one of Reese's friends to come and film. Do you think everyone's ready?"

"Go check," says Thanh Ha.

"Will do! I'll inspect." Reese follows me.

In the section next to ours, Jonah adjusts the vials in the mad scientist's den, as well as a few fake rats. Thanh Ha and Lindsay's zombie section looks ready. And in the front, Samir and the other sixth-grade boys fiddle with a row of battery-operated chattering skeletons.

"They look fakey, which is the point," says Samir. "It'll get the customers to relax, so that they won't be prepared for when we jump out at them from behind the gravestones."

"It's going to look great on film. Is everyone ready?"

"I was born ready," he says from behind the coffin.

My walkie-talkie crackles and I can hear Lindsay exclaim, "Okay, our vampires, Hannah and Ethan, have arrived. Ethan's got his phone out and is ready to film."

"Hannah?" I look at Reese in confusion. "You asked her to film. And Ethan?"

"Yeah. My friends couldn't do it. And Hannah said she'd be happy to. But she didn't have her phone. So she found someone to do it with her. I guess she nabbed Ethan. He's a YouTuber and stuff. Anyway, it made sense since they are tour guides, anyway."

My stomach clenches. Why would Hannah be happy to do anything for me? And why would she bring Ethan?

"Quiet! Into positions," calls out Thanh Ha. "Skeletons behind gravestones!"

Through my walkie-talkie, I can hear Lindsay gush, "Looks like we have a very cute couple."

Couple? What is she talking about? I can hear Hannah sounding fakey and whimpering, "Ethan, hold my hand!" she says. "I'm scared of the dark."

What? Hold her hand?

"They've now entered the first room, the grave-yard," reports Lindsay. "Ethan is filming! They're holding hands so we want to scare them apart."

They need to scare them apart?

My arms shake. I suddenly feel like a volcano that's about to erupt.

Hannah knows I like Ethan. Over the sound effects—moaning, chains, screeching owls—I can hear Hannah's laughter ringing out.

Then there's screaming. Hannah and Ethan both yell as the sixth graders pop out from behind their gravestones.

Finally, after what feels like an eternity of more squeals, "oh no's!" and "I can't look!" Hannah and Ethan arrive in my witch's lair. With the help of some makeup, they both have pale white faces, with dots of blood in the corners of their mouth, which seems to spurt from their fangs. They are wearing matching velvety capes.

"I'm frightened," says Hannah in an exaggerated actressy way.

Hannah is the one who draws goth elves! She draws fairies with daggers with razor-sharp teeth. I know she's not afraid. It's all so she can squish closer to Ethan.

On cue, Reese waddles out in his mummy outfit. "Freshly harvested body parts!" he calls out.

"Yeah," I cackle. "I need more for my brew!"

"Oh no! I'm peeling!" shouts Reese. With an ear-shattering moan, Reese tears off his mummy costume, revealing his demented clown outfit.

He lunges at Hannah and Ethan with a fake rubber dagger. "There's fresh eyeballs right here!" he howls.

Hannah backs away, clutching onto Ethan's arm, all while Ethan films it selfie-style for a moment with his phone. Why is he doing that? This is supposed to be for my mom. Did he not get that part?

All I can think about is that I will forever be able to watch Hannah burying her chin in Ethan's shoulder on YouTube.

Reese laughs like a truly maniacal clown. "I wish to donate my body to science!" he yells. "And to harvest yours! I'll be back." In a flash, he sinks down into a coffin.

Ethan shakes his head. "No, no," he mock cries.

"Dearies," I cackle in my witchy voice. "Put your hands in the brew for a delightful surprise. Squish the eyeballs. The newts. And the frog intestines." I'm supposed to cackle again, only I can't.

Hannah has grabbed Ethan's free hand. The one that's not holding up the camera. Leaning over my brew, she says to Ethan, "You go first."

"Do I have to?" says Ethan. Sighing, he puts his left hand into the pot. "Squishy. And the grapes—excuse me, the eyeballs—are too cold. You guys left them in the freezer too long."

"Here," I say, angrily thrusting out his prize. "For you. Fangs!"

Ethan frowns at it. "Can I have something else?"

Disgusted, I launch a pack of gummy worms at him. "Catch." Of course, he can't. One hand has the camera. And the other hand has been slimed by the brew. Bending down, he picks up the gummy worms.

"Nice," he mumbles, and then appears to strut out of the haunted house, leaving Hannah standing by herself. Why would he do that?

Hannah cups her mouth and calls out, "Wait! I need my protector!"

Oh, throw up. Really? Since when does Hannah need to be rescued by anyone for anything?

"Ethan! Come back!" she pleads.

"I'm just going to film you from here," Ethan says. "It's a better angle."

"Be quiet!" I'm gritting my teeth so hard I think they will turn into dust. "You're not supposed to talk while you film. It's going to ruin it." Not that this video hasn't already been ruined! And I'm starting to feel myself un-crush on Ethan. Like the invisible strings that I had always felt between us are breaking as easily as a spider's web.

I force myself to switch gears.

"Put your hand in the brew, little girl," I cackle and glare at Hannah.

She wrinkles her nose. "Ew. No. It's cold."

"It's cold for those who deserve the cold. For those who are chilly. Do you know what's inside of certain humans?" I lean forward. "Do you, little girl? I'll tell you!" I shake my finger, with its gnarled plastic fake nail. "Guts, that's what! Intestines. Spleen. Worms. That's rights! Lots of humans have worms writhing and crawling inside of them!"

"You're going way off script!" says Hannah.

"So what?!"

Reese sits up in his coffin, his mouth gaping open in surprise.

Ethan crouches down. "Hey, this is going good now. Much more energy."

I shush him. And then lunge at Hannah.

We're now almost nose to nose. "Some humans have no respect for the belongings of others," I howl. "They're nothing but liars and they must pay the price!"

Taking another step back, Hannah's back bumps into a large spiderweb. She shrieks in surprise.

"Don't worry, spiders don't bite," I cackle. "But I might."

Hannah frowns. "You're way too off script! Vampires bite, not witches. You have no idea what you're doing. You are the weakest part of the entire Haunted House."

"No, she's not," says Ethan. "This is getting really good."

"Then what do you think about this?" Reaching down under the table, I grab a vanilla cupcake and hurl it at Hannah.

It hits her square on the forehead. Gobs of rainbow icing mash onto her chin. She shrieks. "What's wrong with you?"

"But you like messes, right? Right!"

Ethan keeps filming. "Awesome!"

"Here, maybe this will make you feel at home!" I throw wonder bars, followed by some brownies. At this point, Reese is just staring at me.

"This is going viral!" exclaims Ethan.

Hannah reaches under the table and launches an entire crumb cake at my head. I duck and it hits the wall. That's when Thanh Ha races up to us and yanks me away from the desserts and Hannah.

Lindsay sprints and grabs Hannah. "Stop it! Turn off your camera, Ethan."

"Got it all!" he yells in triumph. Then he frowns at his phone, noticing it's been caught in our food fight. He wipes off some cream.

Other kids race over to see what's happening.

"It sounded really scary in there," says Samir. "Too bad we missed it."

"Don't worry," says Ethan. "I got it all on camera."

"You better not post that," snips Hannah.

"Yeah," I say, realizing that Hannah and I actually agree on something. For once.

That's when Ms. Petrie bursts into the witch's den. She glares at me and then at Hannah. "What's going on in here?"

"I think Lily and Hannah get the award for scariest attraction," says Reese.

Ethan points to his phone. "I'm posting this on YouTube now."

"Absolutely not!" says Ms. Petrie.

At the same time, Hannah and I both yell out, "NO!"

"Is this all part of a new plan or script?" asks Ms. Petrie.

"Um, not really," I admit.

"Definitely not." Hannah brushes cream off her nose.

"I'm really sorry, Ms. Petrie." I wipe chocolate chips off my chin and brownie bits off my shirt. There's at least a half dozen desserts smeared on the floor.

Ms. Petrie puts her hands on her hips. "This is not acceptable. It's one thing to scare people, but there's absolutely no throwing food."

"It won't stain," I say, in what I hope is a cheerful voice. "It was just the desserts from the cakewalk."

"From the cakewalk?!" Ms. Petrie's eyes grow wide with alarm. "What were they doing in here?"

"Um, for safekeeping so the kids wouldn't snack on them," I say in a small voice.

"So instead you throw them?" says Ms. Petrie, her voice higher than normal.

"I didn't plan for this to happen." Now dozens of kids have gathered in the Haunted House and they are all staring at Hannah and me.

Ms. Petrie shakes her head. "Girls, I'm afraid there are going to be consequences for this. But first this all needs to be cleaned up. And not by the custodial team. Once this is spick-and-span, you two"—she makes dagger eyes at Hannah and me—"are going down to the front office."

"We're so sorry," I say as we sit in the principal's office. "Everything's cleaned up."

Mrs. Rumsky, whose silver hair is fluffed in a perfect halo around her head, purses her lips. "Don't you think it's a little late for *sorry*? Don't you think you should have thought before you threw all of those desserts?"

Ms. Petrie sits on our side of the desk. "Well, only one cake. It appears to be mostly cupcakes and brownies."

Mrs. Rumsky steeples her fingers. "At least that's some good news." Behind her is a poster that reads: IMPOSSIBLE IS NOT A FACT. IT'S AN OPINION. I sure hope it's not a fact that we will get suspended or something. Can you get expelled for throwing vanilla rainbow cupcakes?

After Ms. Petrie recounts the entire incident, Mrs. Rumsky announces that she knows what she wants to do.

"Please don't suspend us," I plead. "We cleaned up really well. You wouldn't know anything ever happened."

"You could lick the floor," adds Hannah. "Don't expel us. Please." She puts her hands together like she's going to pray.

"I know it looked bad," I confess.

"Bad?" Ms. Petrie's eyebrows lift. "How about a total disregard for other people's hard work?"

"We won't ever ever *ever* do it again," I promise.

"I certainly hope not," says Mrs. Rumsky. She taps a stack of papers. Could they be expulsion papers? "You're not expelled," she says, as if she can read my mind. "And you can come back to the festival later, at five p.m. Because your teams do need you. And I understand that you've both been very active on your committee."

Hannah and I both nod.

Mrs. Rumsky picks up her phone. "I will, however, need to call your parents to explain all of this. And you will be staying after school for detention on Monday."

I've never gotten a detention in my life.

"And you will need to replace all of the desserts

that you tossed all over the place," says Ms. Petrie. "With freshly baked goods."

"Oh, I can do that," I say, practically popping out of my chair. "I love to bake! I entered an apple pie in the contest."

Mrs. Rumsky gives Ms. Petrie a knowing look. "Ah, yes, about that," she says. "I'm afraid you'll have to withdraw your pie from the contest." The principal looks at Hannah as well. "Did you enter a pie, too?"

"No," Hannah says in her smallest voice. "I entered, um, a piece of artwork."

"Well, you're disqualified, as well," says Mrs. Rumsky in a final-sounding voice.

Hannah's bottom lip trembles. I think she's about to start bawling, and I know exactly how she feels. I would like to start this day all over again.

"The artwork isn't food," Hannah says.

"It doesn't matter," says Mrs. Rumsky.

"I've won in both sixth and seventh grade," says Hannah, in a pleading voice. "This would be my third year and—"

"Well, someone else will win blue ribbons this year. Because I'm afraid it's not going to either of you two."

Chapter Twenty
NOT EASY AS PIE

At home, Dad's hair—well, what's left of it—sticks straight up. "You and Hannah need to come to the living room." He says it in an eerily calm way, as if part of him has deflated. "We are having a full family discussion *now*."

I'm standing in the kitchen, looking to see what ingredients we have that'll allow us to make a half dozen desserts before five o'clock. Miraculously, we have everything we need since Kimberly had bought so many baking supplies at the beginning of the school year.

"Where's Hannah?" asks Kimberly.

I know exactly where Hannah is. She's in our room,

with her face smooshed into a pillow. "She's still in the bedroom."

"I'm going over there to talk to her." She looks at Dad significantly. "And then we all can talk together as a family."

I watch her walk down the hall, knock, and then slip into the room. I head over to the living room.

"Sit down," says Dad. His tone is still not one I'm used to hearing.

I wave my hands, flashing my green witchy fingernail polish at him, trusting that it will bring on a smile. "Do you like my new look?" He doesn't speak. My dad always speaks. "It's not that bad," I say. "I mean, we didn't hurt anyone. Just food. And we have a ton of flour and chocolate chip pieces. Kimberly bought everything anyone would ever need."

From the bedroom, I hear furious whispering and then an ear-piercing, "No!" Whatever could Kimberly have said to Hannah to get her that upset?

"Are you going to tell Mom?" I ask, hugging my knees. "About, you know, the incident."

"Of course I'm telling your mother, and I'm afraid she'll be very disappointed with you, Lily. I know I am."

Oh, Mom won't just be disappointed. She's going to be mad.

"Sorry, Dad. Really. I've just been stressing about the Haunted House. I guess I lost it or something."

"It's more than stress about some Haunted House and you know it," says Dad. "It's all about your relationship with Hannah. You haven't treated her well for a long time."

"And vice versa. She hasn't exactly been Miss Friendly." Back in the bedroom, there's repeated *no*'s from Hannah and then a firm *yes* from Kimberly.

"It's hard, Lily. This is her house, and she's having to share her mom. And her room."

"What about me? Mom is thousands of miles away. What about that?"

"Of course, I know that's not easy for you. But I expect more from you. Take the higher road." He sighs. "But at the same time, I get it. I really do. I know how much you're missing your mom."

"You sound like a bumper sticker."

"Lily, you're not giving this a chance. There's nothing more important to me than being a family. I can't have you and your stepsister having it out like this at school."

"Like you and Mom got along so well and never went off on each other."

Dad pauses. "That's in the past." He folds his arms in front of his chest. "You know I'm supportive of your mother's education and internship, even though we're no longer . . ." He trails off for a moment. "Together. You need to be supportive of her, too, and that starts with getting along with Hannah. Your mom shouldn't be worrying about this; she should be learning and focusing on her work."

He's right. I know he's right.

"So what are you going to do to me?" I ask. Now it's my turn to feel completely deflated.

"For starters, hand over your phone. No phone for a week, unless your mom calls." I stare at my cell, all warm in my hands, and then reluctantly hand it over. "And you're going to promise me that you'll make a real effort to get along with Hannah from here on out."

"Okay," I say, gritting my teeth. I honestly don't like how Hannah is getting to play the victim here. I'm the nice one! He needs to know the whole story. "She's the one who started the whole thing." And then I explain to Dad pretty much everything that happened from the beginning. Except I leave out the part about hiding Hannah's social studies book. I guess, I feel like it makes me look mean or something.

As Dad listens, he alternates between smiling like he's amused and furrowing his brow, as if some of this stuff makes sense and part of it is new information. "You need to quit this battle with your stepsister—you both do. Next time there's an issue, I want you to feel like you can tell me what's going on. I'm the first to admit that I've been distracted, so I haven't made it easy for you to do that."

"Yeah, well. That's kind of true. You're never really around and you were always bailing on apple picking. I mean, really, every single time."

Dad's face falls. "That's true. I've been too absent. I need to do a better job of being there for you, Lily. And for Hannah. I'm glad you're really telling me how you feel." He sighs. "The whole issue here is that no one is communicating. Everyone's holding back. I've been wound up with my new business, but if you ever need to talk to me, I'm here."

"I know."

"You need to express what you're feeling with words and emotions rather than planning pranks and holding everything in."

"I'll work on that," I tell him. And then decide to start doing so right then. "It's been hard. Okay, like really, really hard, sharing a room with Hannah. She's a mess and pretty grumpy. Almost all the time."

"Well, I'm putting it all together now," he admits. "Sort of. I'm really sorry for putting you in a rough situation with the room sharing. It certainly, in retrospect, maybe wasn't the best idea. What I think is that you all—we all—need to spend some more quality time together. And Kimberly and I've promised each other we're going to plan some fun family weekend outings. Rafting, hiking, biking, going to museums or out to eat." He rubs his hands together, seemingly happy with this solution. But I'm doubtful. Will more time together really help us get along? We already see each other morning, night, and at school.

"So you and Hannah are going to bake now and replace the items you destroyed, okay? At 4:30, I'm driving you back to the Fall Festival, which gives you three hours to get your baking done."

"Great. Mrs. Rumsky said we needed to be at the festival since our committee needs us."

"Yes, that's a good idea." He peers down the hall, toward Hannah's bedroom, and then turns back to me. "We both wanted to have a family conversation about this, but we'll do that later. After everyone has calmed down and once the baking is finished. Maybe after the festival."

Oh no. That thought is semi-terrifying. "You know, at the festival, I'm like the good witch since I give out prizes."

"Well, you better get to the kitchen and get cooking," says Dad. "And do some good!"

The bedroom door opens, and Kimberly and Hannah come out. Hannah slams the door shut with a bang.

She doesn't look or sound happy. At all. It's going to be a long afternoon.

Chapter Twenty-One
SILENCE IS NOT GOLDEN

Baking together is not going well. Mostly because Hannah isn't speaking to me. Plus, she's really not helping much, either. She's mostly sitting around staring at a cookbook, waiting for inspiration. So I start baking for both of us. I try not to think about her holding hands with Ethan or the smug look on her face when she approached the witch's den. Or how she said everything I was doing in the Haunted House was wrong. I try not to think of her at all and just bake.

I've gathered most of the ingredients on the counter. Flour. Baking powder. Eggs. Oil. Butter. Chocolate chips. Cocoa. Vanilla. Confectioner's sugar.

"I thought we'd do batches of brownies," I say. "And then a giant chocolate chip cookie. That's fun."

Hannah says nothing.

I continue talking. "And then cupcakes. In the interest of time, we'll use cake mixes and store-bought icing, versus trying to do a layer cake."

She's glaring at me, actually.

"Okay. Are you going to take credit for my baking, just like you tried to take credit for my note taking?"

"It's all about you and how perfect you are, is that it? You know, you never once asked to look at my drawings," she says.

"That's not true. I asked once. But you were huffy."

"Because of your tone. You said it like an accusation, not like you actually cared. You said it like a prison guard might if an inmate was found scribbling on a cement block."

"What?! I didn't say it like that."

"You did." She drums her fingers on the table.

"I'm sure I didn't say it like that. . . . You make things up." This time I'm saying it intentionally judgy. Now she'll know what I sound like when I get actually mad.

But she laughs at me. "That's the point. I make things up. I create. What do you do?"

"What do I do? I do not leave my dirty dishes on the counter or in the sink, or my dirty clothes on the floor. I do not eat the grapes that someone else carefully washed and pretend that I didn't. I do not dump out your bags and leave all of your belongings on the floor! And even if I did, it's not like you'd be able to notice with the messes you make!" Then I stomp out of the kitchen, only I'm so mad I accidentally end up in the garage and practically bump into the washer and dryer.

When I look on the ground, I notice various items once kept in my backpack are scattered all over Maisie's bed. Mostly wrappers from food that had gone missing. Granola bars. A packet of gum. A bag of chips. And there's a crumpled piece of paper with food stains on it.

Blowing off the crumbs, I examine the paper. It's a portrait of me. And it's really good! With shading and different colors. It looks like me, only a whole lot cooler. Mostly because I have pink hair, elf ears, and wings. It's signed by Hannah, and it says *To Lily* with a little heart. It's dated close to when I moved into the townhouse.

Flying back into the kitchen, I wave the drawing. "What's this?" I ask Hannah. "Did you make this for me?"

She reluctantly nods. "The first day of school when Keisha was over. I was feeling badly about racing you to the shower that morning and wanted to make it up to you. I put it into your backpack."

"Well, I didn't get it . . . but Maisie did." Then I laugh in amazement. "She put it in this hoard along with a bunch of my snacks."

"Do you leave your backpack open?" asks Hannah.

"Yup."

Hannah claps her hand over her mouth. "Oh my gosh. I think Maisie is a thief! I've had stuff taken from my backpack, too. And I thought it was actually you."

That's when I start laughing.

"Now I know why you thought I was going through your backpack." Hannah shakes her head but she's sort of smiling. "Maisie's such a naughty dog."

"Totally," I agree.

Hannah sighs and goes back to her glum face.

"You look really upset," I say.

"My mom grounded me."

"Because of us?"

"Not really. I can't go to GeekGirlCon because of my social studies test grade. I completely flunked it. Normally, I can cram, but without a book, I was in a big trouble. It was fill-in-the-blank, so I had no idea what to write. I just drew sketches of you as Frankenstein's bride. And the teacher PDFed Mom a copy. She was not happy."

"Wow. I'm so sorry, Hannah. . . . I kind of would like to see myself as Frankenstein's bride, though. It might give me some costume ideas for Halloween. But seriously. She won't let you go?"

"Nope! When she told me I was grounded and no GeekGirlCon, I thought my head was going to explode. If my head were in a comic book, it would've taken up an entire splash panel. There would just this one dialogue bubble, 'NOOOOOOOOOOOOOOOOOOOOOOOO OOOOOOOOOOOOOOOOOO!'"

I'm not sure what a splash panel is but I get the idea.

I stand up. "Hannah, there's something that I have to do. Right now. I'll be right back!"

I race into the living room, where Dad and Kimberly, who was forced to come home since the school called her, too, are sitting and reading sections of the newspaper. "Don't punish Hannah," I tell them. "It's not her fault. I hid Hannah's social studies book." I can see Hannah peeking out of the kitchen, her mouth open wide in astonishment.

"You what?" Dad whirls around to stare at me.

"I hid it. It's all my fault. Don't punish her. If I hadn't done that, Hannah would've have been able to study during advisory, and she would've able to get a B-plus or even an A-minus."

"Lily, why would you ever do that?" asks Dad.

"Because I hid her phone," says Hannah, now joining me in the living room.

"Wow," says Kimberly. "It sounds like you girls really do need to work things out. And having very absent parents hasn't helped. We've been preoccupied with trying to get in shape and house hunting. Still, you girls have taken this way too far."

I hang my head. "I know. I'm really super sorry. I've been feeling badly about this for days. I really wanted to say something to Hannah, but I was afraid."

"Well, thanks for saying something now," says Kimberly. "In light of this, I do need to rethink the punishment." She turns to look at her daughter. "Hannah, it's okay for you to go to GeekGirlCon. But it's also not okay for you girls to be sabotaging each other. Both of you need to work on communicating much better." Then she looks imploringly at Hannah. "And, honey, you do need to work on your organization skills. You can't live your life doing everything last minute."

"I know," says Hannah. She steps closer to me and bumps my shoulder. "There's a lot I can learn from Lily."

Wow. Did I really just hear that?

"Look, I know I told Lily we'd wait until after the festival," says Dad, "but I think we should talk now." He points to the couch. "Why don't you both sit down and we'll stand?"

"Sort of swap places," finishes Kimberly.

Now Hannah and I look at each other in confusion. What could this be about? It seems like more than just Hannah and I not getting along.

When Dad and Kimberly stand in front of us, they look like a united wall of parents.

Dad begins, "So it's not like Kimberly and I have been blind to the tension between the two of you. In fact, it's been, frankly, hard not to notice when quarters are so tight."

"It's part of the reason we've so busy looking for a new house, for all of us," continues Kimberly. "We've just been trying to be real patient because we know it's rough all around." She glances at my dad. "Brad has wanted to say something about the atmosphere being created for a long time, but I've been urging him to let you work it out on your own. We both noticed that in the past couple of days you seemed to be getting along better."

"But then the phone call from the school didn't make us too happy," adds Dad.

"I'm really sorry about you girls getting disqualified from the contests," says Kimberly. "But I think it was the right decision."

"Definitely," says Dad. "It's one thing for you two not to get along, but for it to spill over into school like that." Dad shakes his head.

"But there's something else," says Kimberly. "But this doesn't feel like the right time discuss it."

Both Hannah and I look at our parents.

"Is it bad?" I ask as Hannah nods.

"It's not bad," says Dad. "I think you all might be happily surprised. But"—he glances at his phone—"you're running out of time. Looks like you girls have a baking job to do in the kitchen. So get cooking!'

I look at Hannah and she looks at me, and both of us race into the kitchen. Soon we are stirring and mixing and measuring.

"I wish we had two ovens," I say. "We're going to have to be creative to get everything to fit into the oven."

"I'm good spatially," says Hannah. And within minutes, she somehow wedges all of our cakes and cookies into the oven. They are definitely not going to bake evenly with everything in the oven at once, but right now I need to let go of being a perfectionist.

"That's a miracle," I say. "Wow." I pause. "Look. I'm really sorry, Hannah. About everything."

"Me too. I want to explain why I was acting so cold the day you moved in." She takes a deep breath. "I had to clear out my paints to make way for your dresser and take down my art, and some photos, including some of my dad. Also, around the house, Mom had taken down all of Dad's photos. It happened over time when Mom started to date. I had always been promised that this was going to be our home forever. My dad died suddenly of a heart attack when I was three, and this house is all that I have left of him. I can barely remember him, except through photos."

I can't imagine not remembering what my parents look like. Needing a photo in order to remember. I close my eyes, and I can see my mom's long brown hair and her freckled nose. But it's not like having her there. I would be so sad if I couldn't pull up her image in my mind.

"It's okay if you put up some photos of him in our room," I say.

"That would be nice," she says. "I just didn't want to make your dad feel bad."

"It's funny but I had put up a ton of photos of Mom and I hadn't considered your mom's feelings."

"Oh, she's fine with it," says Hannah. "You're lucky to have such a nice dad."

"Yeah. Even if he's a little busy."

"Yes, still."

"He's your dad, too. Well, stepdad."

"Thanks for saying that." Hannah pauses. "There's something you have to know about the committee. I got on the Haunted House committee because I really wanted to be able to use my love of art and theater to help the festival. It wasn't to get at you. Not at first, anyway."

"Plus, you knew about my crush on Ethan,"

"Well, it would be hard not to. I did also overhear, but it didn't mean anything at the time. I've known Ethan since forever from swim team. And he's okay. But he can be a somewhat of a jerk. He's the kind of person who texts other people when he's with you, and then when you're the person not with him, you feel badly because he's with someone else." She shakes her head.

"I could kind of tell. I mean, not right away. But, gradually, that, maybe, he isn't always so nice."

"He's not bad. I mean, he's fun. When I was leaning over him at the house, I was looking at his phone, watching one of his lame YouTube videos. But then I saw your upset expression and there was a little bit of me that enjoyed irritating you. I'm sorry." She frowns. "I could never actually like Ethan. He's too self-centered."

"But what about at the Haunted House?"

"I was so mad at you for hiding my textbook, and then getting me in trouble for skipping swim practice, so I wanted to get you really upset. When Reese asked me to film, I told him that I didn't have a phone, so I just asked Ethan to do it instead. And tried to pretend I liked him. I'm really sorry. It wasn't cool."

"Agreed," I say.

"But something good has happened from it. Mom and I had a huge discussion about why I skipped swim team. And I told her I feel like I have no free time. Every day, I'm doing something. So we talked about me finding another swim team. Something less competitive. Maybe just join a gym where I could free swim."

"Wow. But you have so many ribbons in swimming."

"Yeah, but ribbons aren't everything. I really like art. Even more than theater. Speaking of theater, you were a pretty scary witch."

"Thanks."

"I mean, you really were good. You should maybe look into it. I think Ms. Petrie mentioned she's opened to doing an improv group. Reese would be good at it, too."

"Yeah, he probably would," I admit.

For a moment, we sit in silence, and then I notice Hannah's iPad in the corner of the table. "Would you mind telling me what do you do on your iPad all day? I mean, I know you sketch. But I often see you making these flowers. I know it's something"—I pause—"cool. But I have no idea how you do it."

Hannah's face brightens. "So what I do is draw a flower. At first when I didn't know flowers so well, I needed reference drawings, so I went online to find them. Then I loaded them into this software program and crossbred them."

"Wow, that sounds complicated."

"Not really. Seriously, the program does all the work. It's like breeding tropical fish. I get to pick out the features I like the most."

"Imagine if you could do that for boys." We both laugh.

Then Hannah glances over at my planner, sticking out of my backpack against the wall. "Look, I could use your help being a little more organized. Maybe I could get a day planner and you could show me how it works."

"Sure!" I say, excited to show Hannah my love for all-things-planners.

"And I noticed you have special stickers for it. I could show you how to make your own."

"Really? That'd be awesome!"

"Yeah, there's this app where you can make anything into a sticker. Photos of your friends. Ice cream. You can draw it yourself or use a photo. Like one of Maisie." When Hannah says Maisie's name, the dog comes trotting over to both of us. "Since you've moved in, she's gotten so much better."

"Yeah," I say. "But she's still naughty."

"An opportunist." Hannah rubs Maisie's belly. "You see a backpack and then you had to scavenge, didn't you?"

Poor Maisie is desperate to lick the mixing bowls. "No sweets for you, Maisie Waisie," says Hannah. "It's bad for your little doggy stomach."

Then suddenly, I get an idea. "We could work with her," I say. "Maybe take an obedience class together." I giggle. "I mean Maisie would take the obedience class and we would go with her."

"Actually," says Hannah, "we both could probably use one." We both laugh, then finish our baking, and the whole house smells sweet and delicious.

Chapter Twenty-Two
MAGIC MOMENTS

Before I leave for the Fall Festival, I quickly text Keisha to let her know that I made up with Hannah. And to also apologize for not doing a very good job at storing the desserts for the cakewalk. I also apologize to Keisha for not supporting her while I was scheming against Hannah, and she accepts my apology.

She texts me that she loves me, even if I got into a little food fight.

Although it's super late in Morocco, I video chat with Mom. Dad has filled her in on everything. She tells me that she's so glad that Hannah and I are now working it out, and that she believed we always could.

"I'm sorry that you're not going to be able to enter the pie, Lily," she says.

"Me too. But there's always next year."

"I like the way you're thinking. Hey, I've been learning so many cool things about Morocco. I wanted to share just a few fun facts. Did you know which country was the very first one in the whole world to recognize the United States?"

"I have a feeling it might be, um, Morocco."

"Bingo!" Mom claps her hands. "And did you know that people have lived in Morocco for over ninety thousand years?"

"Whoa! That's a long time."

"And here's the most important fact of all. Remember how I told you that Morocco is really famous for argan oil?"

"Not exactly," I admit.

"Well, it's this amazing oil, which has become quite valuable. Because it's, for one, supposed to work wonders on your hair and skin." Mom pats her cheek. "I've been using it, and I've noticed that my skin's so much smoother and less dry. But here's the thing. Traditionally, argan oil is helped along by goat poop."

I start laughing. "Mom, are you serious?"

"Completely. The goats jump into argan trees. You should see them. It's quite a sight, all of these goats balanced on various branches. Anyway, the goats chow down on the fruit, then poop out the nuts. Then the farmers use the nuts to extract the oil. That means they take something that's literally poop and, basically, turn it into something a bit like gold."

"Okaaaaaay."

"What I'm getting at is that something that seems kind of unpleasant can—"

"Be turned into fertilizer?"

"Well, sure, you can look at it that way, too."

"I think I see what you mean."

"So when I come back in December, I'm definitely bringing you some argan oil."

"December? What? I thought you were away for a year!"

"I am, but I'm going to come home for the holidays, for a week and a half." Mom is jumping up and down, and I'm jumping up and down, too.

"Mom, that's amazing news."

"I know. So we have a date, then, to bake some pies."

"Yes, definitely!" I shout. "I love you, Mom."

"And I love you, too, Babu."

"Shhh," I say, putting my fingers to my lips. "Nobody around here knows that nickname, and I don't want to break it to them, because I'll never it live it down."

She blows me a kiss, and just like that, it's time to leave to go to the Fall Festival.

The festival will officially start in fifteen minutes. Everyone is supposed to get into position for when the crowds are allowed inside. As Hannah and I make our way toward the Haunted House, I see Ethan with his friend Josh, only I notice how he's only half paying attention to him. His eyes are constantly down on his phone. I realize now that I was more into the idea of Ethan than the real Ethan, who might look mature, but he's not really. He doesn't really listen well. And he's mostly just into himself. And his YouTube channel.

Both Hannah and I say hi when we pass by him, and then we roll our eyes.

I stroll past the cakewalk and wave to Keisha. "I see my dad dropped off the desserts," I say as she tidies up the line of desserts.

She nods. "I was really worried that all of the cake-walk desserts were going to be history. Thank you so much for making new ones."

"Of course. I'm really sorry about the food fight. It was just . . . well, you know, not a good idea."

"Yeah, well, you've given everyone something to talk about."

"Really? So everyone at school knows?"

"Pretty much." Keisha fiddles with some of the plastic wrap around a Bundt cake. "But at least you made up with Hannah. Honestly, it was driving me crazy. It was all you ever talked about. Well, that and Ethan."

"Yeah," I admit. "Well, I'm over him now. I did get a little obsessed. Both with Ethan and pranking Hannah. Ugh."

"Well, I can't imagine what it must be like knowing your mom is so far away."

"Good news," I report. "Mom's coming back for winter break! Ten whole days."

Keisha give me a hug. "Really? That's awesome news!"

"And I'll try to come to your next skating competition. I really want to cheer you on."

"That would be nice. They can be a little boring, all that waiting around."

"Yeah. You're worth it, though. Plus, I get to see Quinn." Keisha grins.

Soon afterward, I skip past the contest in the so-called barn, which is really just a bunch of cardboard painted red and cut out like a barn, with bales of hay in front.

The pies sit on all the tables now in the barn area. My heart sinks a little. Mine isn't there, of course. I gave my apple pie away to the cakewalk. My eyes peer at the far wall, where the art contest is.

Hannah's drawing isn't there either. It's sad, but at the same time, the food fight, in a weird way, helped me make up with Hannah.

The time in the Haunted House whizzes by and everyone has so much fun. Dad and Kimberly even go through twice!

After a couple of hours, Ms. Petrie pops into the witch's den during a lull and tells Reese and me that we should take a twenty-minute break to enjoy the festival ourselves. And that we all should close the

Haunted House, just for a little bit. Ms. Petrie leaves to tell the others on the Haunted House committee.

With our costumes still on, Reese and I exit out the back. "The little kids sure love their gummy worms," I say.

"I know," he says, pulling off his clown nose and crazy orange wig.

It seems like everyone is going around the festival wearing their plastic fangs. "It's like a school full of vampires," I say to Reese. "From what I can tell, the Haunted House was extra popular this year. I wish I knew what it was like as a customer."

"Hey, do you want to go and walk in together?" asks Reese.

"Really? But it's closed."

He nods. "I know but we would still get some of the experience."

When we get to the front, Lindsay stands with a walkie-talkie, and we explain what we want to do.

"Hey, everyone is still here," she says. "If you two hustle on through now, you'll get to experience everything, except, obviously, the witch's den, since, well, you're here. And not in there."

"Sure, let's do it!" I cry.

"Ready?" Reese asks, pointing to the front entrance.

"Ready!" I nod.

"Are you frightened?"

"Even though I know where the scares are? Maybe just a little bit," I admit.

"Me too." He peers at me shyly and offers his hand.

I take it, and his hand feels warm and nice. I'm holding a boy's hand! A cute boy. A boy that makes me laugh.

He smiles and his famous dimples appear. Wow, he really is cute. I can admit that without hesitation now. "So you want to know why I call you Magic?" he asks.

"Because I'm magical?"

He laughs. "Remember in sixth grade when Magic 8 Balls were all the rage?"

"Oh yeah." I giggle.

"You'd ask it everything. What you were going to eat for dessert, whether someone was going to come to your slumber party, and what boy from your class you were going to marry. It was ridiculous."

I feel my face warm a little bit but let him continue.

"Well, at a slumber party you went to—" he starts

to blush now—"apparently, you asked the Magic 8 Ball about me. Whether I'm your crush or something."

"Oh gosh, I remember that." We had all been goofing around. And I was pretty much asking as a joke.

"It said, 'My reply is no' or maybe it was 'Outlook not so good.' Well, someone—I won't say who—told me about it. About how you liked Magic 8 Balls. And, well, ever since I've called you Magic."

"Wait, lots of girls asked the Magic 8 about guys. Not just me. And I'm pretty sure other girls asked about you, as well. I guess I don't get it." I'm definitely confused.

"Well, maybe I asked about you, specifically. Maybe I asked who you asked the Magic 8 Ball about."

"Really?" I say, and we're still holding hands and it's all coming to me. Reese has had a crush on me since sixth grade! That is crazy! And suddenly I feel crazy happy!

"Hey, Luke won your apple pie," he says, right before we step inside the entrance. And we are still holding hands.

"Really? Luke?"

"Yeah. Well, his little sister did. But we both tasted a slice right after Luke won it." He leans in close to me, and he lets go of my hand. "I probably have pie breath."

"That's probably the best kind of breath."

"Yeah, because your pie is really good."

"Thanks," I say. "My mom taught me how to do it."

"She must be a really good baker."

"She is."

"I love cooking shows," says Reese. "Especially when they make desserts."

"Same!"

"Maybe we could watch some episodes together."

"That would be fun. . . . And, Reese? If you get scared, I'll protect you." I hold up my hand, the one that he was just holding. "I promise." He retakes my hand and squeezes it gently.

Together, we duck into the Haunted House.

Later, Dad, Kimberly, Hannah, and I are all sitting at a picnic table under an overhang, eating slices of pizza. We're wearing our raincoats since it's drizzling now and very misty. The green makeup runs off my face from time to time.

Dad finishes chewing. "I've been promising apple picking for weeks. And each week I've had to put it off. It's not right." He looks at Kimberly. "We're both so preoccupied. But, Lily, we'll go next weekend."

"That's awesome, Dad. And I don't think that Hannah and Kimberly have ever been. I definitely want to do a father-daughter thing sometime soon, but it might be nice if all of us went."

"I would love that!" says Kimberly.

"Me too," says Hannah, wiping her mouth with a napkin.

"And we'll have the time to go because . . . we've found a house!" announces Dad.

"You have?" I say, genuinely surprised. It seems like Dad and Kimberly were just going to look forever.

"Is it in the same neighborhood?" asks Hannah, her brows furrowed in concern. I suddenly remember how attached she is to the townhouse. "Will we go to the same school?"

"I hope so," I say, since I can't imagine being separated from Keisha or any of my other friends right now.

"Well," says Dad, "you will absolutely go to the same school. And the house is some place verrrrrry familiar. Someplace you know well."

"Where?" I try to think of a house I know well. It's not like any of my friends' houses are up for sale.

Kimberly knocks on the picnic table. "We're staying at the townhouse. We're not moving. That's the good surprise we wanted to tell you about earlier."

Hannah and I look at each other in shock.

"In the end, Brad and I decided we should wait another few years until he pays off his business loan." Kimberly smiles. "However, the way things are going, that won't be long."

"Plus," continues Dad, "Kimberly was just promoted in her job. Not just administrative coordinator for the communications department, but the head of *all* of the administrative coordinators at the University of Washington, Tacoma."

"Way to go, Mom!" Hannah and I both high-five Kimberly.

"So we've decided to fix up the townhouse," explains Kimberly. "New kitchen. And we'll convert the office into Lily's bedroom."

"We've also just hired a contractor to help us renovate the basement," says Dad, "which has been neglected for too long. I'll have my office down there, and the rest of the space we'll use as a recreation/family room for you girls. There will be enough room for a ping-pong table and an art table for Hannah. Plus, practice space for Lily to play her flute."

"But where will you store your video equipment if the downstairs is going to be a rec room?" I ask.

"Drumroll please," Dad says. "When we were looking for houses, we came across a loft space downtown. And I signed a lease. Tacoma Sports Films has a new home!"

"Wow, an office!" I exclaim. "Dad, you'll have a regular job in a regular office."

"I know—it's a miracle. But this is different. It will be *my* office."

I pop off the bench to hug Dad. The rain is starting to come down harder now.

"I'm so happy for you. For us." I pause and I can feel something stretching inside of me. In a good kind of way. "For my family."

A few minutes later, when Dad and Kimberly go up to order some apple cider from the refreshment stand, Hannah and I marvel about no longer having to share a room.

"I'm going to miss your alarm clock," confesses Hannah. "The crazy bleeping."

"And I'm going to miss the pile of clothes I have to walk around."

"Actually, in a weird way, it will be too quiet having my own room."

"I know," I say.

"Maybe sometimes we can have a sleepover. In each other's rooms. I'll show you the flower cross-breeding program. And you can name your new species."

"And maybe I can help you hang some of your awesome drawings in your room. And in mine, too. If we get someone in the family to go to IKEA, we can get some frames."

"That'd be great. I'm glad you're into it." She pauses. "Next time I feel like you're being all judgy because I'm wasting my time doing art, I'll say something and we'll work it out."

"Definitely," I agree and then it's my turn to pause. "I promise the next time I feel like you're acting kind of like a bully, I'm going to say something." I put my hand over my heart and it's racing but only a little. "Wow. That was weird to be so real like that."

"But good weird, right?"

"Uh-huh. Good and weird and right." I talked about my feelings and didn't combust into flames or something.

"Your cider awaits," says Dad, setting some mugs down onto the table. The apple cider smells sweet and tart—just delicious. Kimberly also sets down a paper plate with some honey-glazed donuts. The rain is coming down harder now, but it's all good. Nothing we're not used to!

At that moment, my phone beeps. It's a text from Reese, which makes me smile.

I hold up my cider and so do Dad and Kimberly, and we toast to family, apple pies, elves, flower drawings, and many more adventures to come. We are going to live like the mountain is out.

SWIRL

Pumpkin Spice Secrets

by Hillary Homzie

Sometimes secrets aren't so sweet . . .

When Maddie spills her pumpkin spice drink on a cute boy, she's instantly smitten. But add best friend drama and major school stress to Maddie's secret coffee shop crush, and it's a recipe for disaster. Can she stay true to both her friend and her heart?

Sky Pony Press
New York

SWIRL

Peppermint Cocoa Crushes

by Laney Nielson

Friends, cocoa, crushes . . . catastrophe!

'Tis the season for snow, gifts, peppermint cocoa, and the school's variety show competition! But Sasha's head is spinning between rehearsals, homework, and volunteer commitments. Can she make the most of her moment in the spotlight?

Sky Pony Press
New York

SWIRL

Cinnamon Bun Besties

by Stacia Deutsch

It's bestie vs. bestie . . .

When the Valentine's Day fund-raiser Suki is running gets out of control and the local animal shelter where she volunteers is in danger of closing, she's determined to save the day. But she can't do it alone—and her only hope for help is her worst enemy . . .

Sky Pony Press
New York

SWIRL

Salted Caramel Dreams

by Jackie Nastri Bardenwerper

Friendship without drama? Dream on!

Jasmine has always been best friends with Kiara. They have a secret handshake, a plan to open a joint Etsy shop, and even invented a salted caramel drink together at the local cafe. But when Kiara joins the basketball team, she starts to become distant . . . and then she betrays Jasmine's trust.

Sky Pony Press
New York

SWIRL

Apple Pie Promises
by Hillary Homzie

A new stepsister, an old crush, and the best Fall Festival of all time. Bring on the drama!

Lily's mom has gotten a once-in-a-lifetime work opportunity in Africa and will be gone for a year, so Lily is moving in with her dad—and new stepmom and stepsister—right in time for the Fall Festival. Sharing a bedroom is one thing, but sharing a crush is another . . .

Sky Pony Press
New York

SWIRL

Cotton Candy Wishes
by Kristina Springer

Is achieving the social status of your dreams really all that sweet?

When Taylor's dad gets a new job and they move to a new town, Taylor gets the chance to reinvent herself as one of the popular kids. At first, all her dreams are coming true! But she soon realizes that being with the in-crowd isn't what she thought it would be.

Sky Pony Press
New York

About the Author

Hillary Homzie is the author of the tween novels *Queen of Likes*, *The Hot List*, and *Things Are Gonna Get Ugly*, as well as the comedic chapter book series Alien Clones From Outer Space. During the summers, Hillary teaches in the graduate program in children's writing at Hollins University. A former sketch comedy performer in New York City, Hillary currently lives with her family in Northern California.